Date Due

BRODART, CO.   Cat. No. 23-233-003   Printed in U.S.A.

CAREER IDEAS
for kids who like
TRAVEL

DIANE LINDSEY REEVES
AND
GAYLE BRYAN

Illustrations by
NANCY BOND

Ferguson
An imprint of ☑ Facts On File

CAREER IDEAS FOR KIDS WHO LIKE TRAVEL

Copyright © 2001 by Diane Lindsey Reeves

Ferguson
An imprint of Facts On File, Inc.
132 West 31st Street
New York NY 10001

Library of Congress Cataloging-in-Publication Data

Reeves, Diane Lindsey, 1959–
      Career ideas for kids who like travel / Diane Lindsey Reeves
and Gayle Bryan; illustrations by Nancy Bond.
          p.   cm. — (Career ideas for kids who like)
      Includes bibliographical references and index.
      ISBN 0-8160-4325-6
          1. Vocational guidance—Juvenile literature. 2. Employment in
      foreign countries—Juvenile literature. [1. Tourism—Vocational guidance.
      2. Vocational guidance.]
      I. Bryan, Gayle. II. Bond, Nancy, ill. III. Title.

HF5381.2.R4288 2001
331.7'02—dc21   00-069513

Ferguson books are available at special discounts when purchased in bulk quantities for businesses, associations, institutions or sales promotions. Please call our Special Sales Department in New York at 212/967-8800 or 800/322-8755.

You can find Ferguson on the World Wide Web at http://www.fergpubco.com

Text and cover design by Smart Graphics
Illustrations by Nancy Bond

This book is printed on acid-free paper.

Printed in the United States of America

MP FOF 10 9 8 7 6 5 4

To my readers, young and old,
with high hopes and best wishes for a future of
chances taken and dreams fulfilled.
—DLR

 ACKNOWLEDGMENTS

A million thanks to those who took the time to invest in young lives by sharing their stories about work and providing photos for this book:

Michelle Abrete
Douglas Allen
Donna Brown
Lisa Connacher
Susan Dziama
Clyde George
Jon Goodman
Kirby Green
Shelley Gumucio
Bernard Hamburger
Mike Hamburger
Michael Harney
Chuck Hunter
Deborah Joyce
Shelley Matheny
Alison Smale

Also, special thanks to the design team of Smart Graphics, Nancy Bond, and Cathy Rincon for bringing the Career Ideas for Kids series to life with their creative talent.

Finally, much appreciation and admiration is due to my editor, Nicole Bowen, whose vision and attention to detail increased the quality of this project in many wonderful ways.

CONTENTS

MAKE A CHOICE!

You're young. Most of your life is still ahead of you. How are you supposed to know what you want to be when you grow up?

You're right: 10, 11, 12, 13 is a bit young to know exactly what and where and how you're going to do whatever it is you're going to do as an adult. But, it's the perfect time to start making some important discoveries about who you are, what you like to do, and what you do best. It's the ideal time to start thinking about what you *want* to do.

Make a choice! If you get a head start now, you may avoid setbacks and mistakes later on.

When it comes to picking a career, you've basically got two choices.

CHOICE A

Wait until you're in college to start figuring out what you want to do. Even then you still may not decide what's up your alley, so you graduate and jump from job to job still searching for something you really like.

Hey, it could work. It might be fun. Lots of (probably most) people do it this way.

The problem is that if you pick Choice A, you may end up settling for second best. You may miss out on a meaningful education, satisfying work, and the rewards of a focused and well-planned career.

You have another choice to consider.

CHOICE B

Start now figuring out your options and thinking about the things that are most important in your life's work: Serving others? Staying true to your values? Making lots of money? Enjoying your work? Your young years are the perfect time to mess around with different career ideas without messing up your life.

Reading this book is a great idea for kids who choose B. It's a first step toward choosing a career that matches your skills, interests, and lifetime goals. It will help you make a plan for tailoring your junior and high school years to fit your career dreams. To borrow a jingle from the U.S. Army—using this book is a way to discover how to "be all that you can be."

Ready for the challenge of Choice B? If so, read the next section to find out how this book can help start you on your way.

HOW TO USE THIS BOOK

This isn't a book about interesting careers that other people have. It's a book about interesting careers that you can have.

Of course, it won't do you a bit of good to just read this book. To get the whole shebang, you're going to have to jump in with both feet, roll up your sleeves, put on your thinking cap—whatever it takes—to help you do these three things:

- 💡 **Discover** what you do best and enjoy the most. (This is the secret ingredient for finding work that's perfect for you.)

☼ **Explore** ways to match your interests and abilities with career ideas.

☼ **Experiment** with lots of different ideas until you find the ideal career. (It's like trying on all kinds of hats to see which ones fit!)

Use this book as a road map to some exciting career destinations. Here's what to expect in the chapters that follow.

GET IN GEAR!

First stop: self-discovery. These activities will help you uncover important clues about the special traits and abilities that make you *you*. When you are finished you will have developed a personal Skill Set that will help guide you to career ideas in the next chapter.

TAKE A TRIP!

Next stop: exploration. Cruise down the career idea highway and find out about a variety of career ideas that are especially appropriate for people who like travel. Use the Skill Set chart at the beginning of each entry to match your own interests with those required for success on the job.

CONDUCT A DETOUR THAT TAKES YOU PLACES!

Here's your chance to see the world through careers in the booming travel and hospitality industries as well as other jobs that can take you places.

Just when you thought you'd seen it all, here come dozens of travel-related ideas to add to the career mix. Charge up your career search by learning all you can about some of these opportunities.

DON'T STOP NOW!

Third stop: experimentation. The library, the telephone, a computer, and a mentor—four keys to a successful career planning adventure. Use them well, and before long you'll be on the trail of some hot career ideas.

WHAT'S NEXT?

Make a plan! Chart your course (or at least the next stop) with these career planning road maps. Whether you're moving full steam ahead with a great idea or get slowed down at a yellow light of indecision, these road maps will keep you moving forward toward a great future.

Use a pencil—you're bound to make a detour or two along the way. But, hey, you've got to start somewhere.

HOORAY! YOU DID IT!

Some final rules of the road before sending you off to new adventures.

SOME FUTURE DESTINATIONS

This section lists a few career planning tools you'll want to know about.

You've got a lot of ground to cover in this phase of your career planning journey. Start your engines and get ready for an exciting adventure!

GET IN GEAR!

Career planning is a lifelong journey. There's usually more than one way to get where you're going, and there are often some interesting detours along the way. But, you have to start somewhere. So, rev up and find out all you can about you—one-of-a-kind, specially designed you. That's the first stop on what can be the most exciting trip of your life!

To get started, complete the two exercises described below.

WATCH FOR SIGNS ALONG THE WAY

Road signs help drivers figure out how to get where they want to go. They provide clues about direction, road conditions, and safety. Your career road signs will provide clues about who you are, what you like, and what you do best. These clues can help you decide where to look for the career ideas that are best for you.

Complete the following statements to make them true for you. There are no right or wrong answers. Jot down the response that describes you best. Your answers will provide important clues about career paths you should explore.

Please Note: If this book does not belong to you, write your responses on a separate sheet of paper.

On my last report card, I got the best grade in _____.

On my last report card, I got the worst grade in _____.

I am happiest when _____.

Something I can do for hours without getting bored is _____.

Something that bores me out of my mind is _____.

My favorite class is _____.

My least favorite class is _____.

The one thing I'd like to accomplish with my life is _____.

My favorite thing to do after school is _.

My least favorite thing to do after school is _____.

Something I'm really good at is _____.

Something that is really tough for me to do is _____.

My favorite adult person is _____ because _____.

When I grow up _____.

The kinds of books I like to read are about _____.

The kinds of videos I like to watch are about _____.

GET SOME DIRECTION

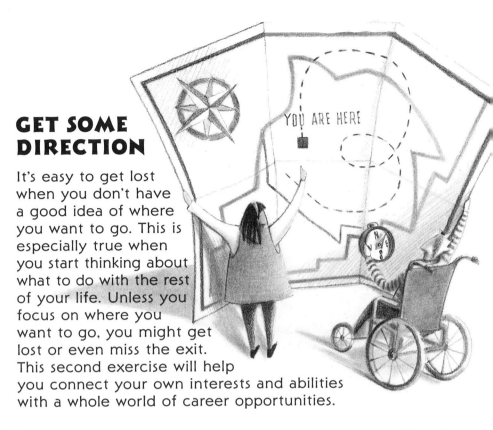

It's easy to get lost when you don't have a good idea of where you want to go. This is especially true when you start thinking about what to do with the rest of your life. Unless you focus on where you want to go, you might get lost or even miss the exit. This second exercise will help you connect your own interests and abilities with a whole world of career opportunities.

Mark the activities that you enjoy doing or would enjoy doing if you had the chance. Be picky. Don't mark ideas that you wish you would do, mark only those that you would really do. For instance, if the idea of skydiving sounds appealing, but you'd never do it because you are terrified of heights, don't mark it.

Please Note: If this book does not belong to you, write your responses on a separate sheet of paper.

- ❏ 1. Rescue a cat stuck in a tree
- ❏ 2. Visit the pet store every time you go to the mall
- ❏ 3. Paint a mural on the cafeteria wall
- ❏ 4. Send e-mail to a "pen pal" in another state
- ❏ 5. Survey your classmates to find out what they do after school
- ❏ 6. Run for student council
- ❏ 7. Try out for the school play
- ❏ 8. Dissect a frog and identify the different organs
- ❏ 9. Play baseball, soccer, football, or _____ (fill in your favorite sport)

❏ 10. Talk on the phone to just about anyone who will talk back

❏ 11. Try foods from all over the world—Thailand, Poland, Japan, etc.

❏ 12. Write poems about things that are happening in your life

❏ 13. Create a really scary haunted house to take your friends through on Halloween

❏ 14. Recycle all your family's trash

❏ 15. Bake a cake and decorate it for your best friend's birthday

❏ 16. Simulate an imaginary flight through space on your computer screen

❏ 17. Build model airplanes, boats, dollhouses, or anything from kits

❏ 18. Sell enough advertisements for the school yearbook to win a trip to Walt Disney World

❏ 19. Teach your friends a new dance routine

❏ 20. Watch the stars come out at night and see how many constellations you can find

❏ 21. Watch baseball, soccer, football, or _____ (fill in your favorite sport) on TV

❏ 22. Give a speech in front of the entire school

❏ 23. Plan the class field trip to Washington, D.C.

❏ 24. Read everything in sight, including the back of the cereal box

❏ 25. Figure out "who dunnit" in a mystery story

❏ 26. Take in stray or hurt animals

❏ 27. Make a poster announcing the school football game

❏ 28. Put together a multimedia show for a school assembly using music and lots of pictures and graphics

❏ 29. Think up a new way to make the lunch line move faster and explain it to the cafeteria staff

❏ 30. Invest your allowance in the stock market and keep track of how it does

❏ 31. Go to the ballet or opera every time you get the chance

❏ 32. Do experiments with a chemistry set

❏ 33. Keep score at your sister's Little League game

❏ 34. Use lots of funny voices when reading stories to children

❏ 35. Ride on airplanes, trains, boats—anything that moves

❏ 36. Interview the new exchange student for an article in the school newspaper

❏ 37. Build your own treehouse

❏ 38. Help clean up a waste site in your neighborhood

❏ 39. Visit an art museum and pick out your favorite painting

❏ 40. Make a chart on the computer to show how much soda students buy from the school vending machines each week

❏ 41. Keep track of how much your team earns to buy new uniforms

❏ 42. Play Monopoly® in an all-night championship challenge

❏ 43. Play an instrument in the school band or orchestra

❏ 44. Put together a 1,000-piece puzzle

❏ 45. Write stories about sports for the school newspaper

❏ 46. Listen to other people talk about their problems

❏ 47. Imagine yourself in exotic places

❏ 48. Hang around bookstores and libraries

❏ 49. Play harmless practical jokes on April Fools' Day

❏ 50. Join the 4-H club at your school
❏ 51. Take photographs at the school talent show
❏ 52. Create an imaginary city using a computer
❏ 53. Do 3-D puzzles
❏ 54. Make money by setting up your own business—paper route, lemonade stand, etc.
❏ 55. Keep track of the top 10 songs of the week
❏ 56. Train your dog to do tricks
❏ 57. Make play-by-play announcements at the school football game
❏ 58. Answer the phones during a telethon to raise money for orphans
❏ 59. Be an exchange student in another country
❏ 60. Write down all your secret thoughts and favorite sayings in a journal
❏ 61. Jump out of an airplane (with a parachute, of course)
❏ 62. Plant and grow a garden in your backyard (or windowsill)
❏ 63. Use a video camera to make your own movies
❏ 64. Spend your summer at a computer camp learning lots of new computer programs
❏ 65. Build bridges, skyscrapers, and other structures out of LEGO®s

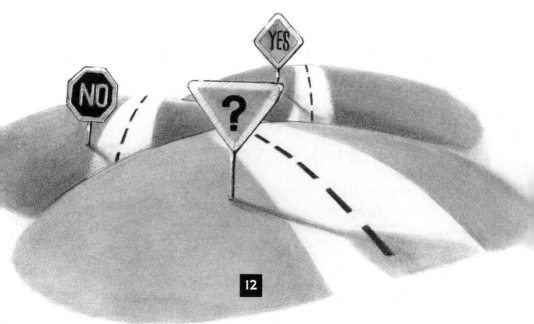

❏ 66. Get your friends together to help clean up your town after a hurricane

❏ 67. Plan a concert in the park for little kids

❏ 68. Collect different kinds of rocks

❏ 69. Help plan a sports tournament

❏ 70. Be DJ for the school dance

❏ 71. Learn how to fly a plane or sail a boat

❏ 72. Write funny captions for pictures in the school yearbook

❏ 73. Scuba dive to search for buried treasure

❏ 74. Recognize and name several different breeds of cats, dogs, and other animals

❏ 75. Sketch pictures of your friends

❏ 76. Pick out neat stuff to sell at the school store

❏ 77. Answer your classmates' questions about how to use the computer

❏ 76. Draw a map showing how to get to your house from school

❏ 79. Make up new words to your favorite songs

❏ 80. Take a hike and name the different kinds of trees, birds, or flowers

❏ 81. Referee intramural basketball games

❏ 82. Join the school debate team

❏ 83. Make a poster with postcards from all the places you went on your summer vacation

❏ 84. Write down stories that your grandparents tell you about when they were young

CALCULATE THE CLUES

Now is your chance to add it all up. Each of the 12 boxes on these pages contains an interest area that is common to both your world and the world of work. Follow these directions to discover your personal Skill Set:

1. Find all of the numbers that you checked on pages 9–13 in the boxes below and X them. Work your way all the way through number 84.
2. Go back and count the Xs marked for each interest area. Write that number in the space that says "total."
3. Find the interest area with the highest total and put a number one in the "Rank" blank of that box. Repeat this process for the next two highest scoring areas. Rank the second highest as number two and the third highest as number three.
4. If you have more than three strong areas, choose the three that are most important and interesting to you.

Remember: If this book does not belong to you, write your responses on a separate sheet of paper.

ADVENTURE	ANIMALS & NATURE	ART
❑ 1	❑ 2	❑ 3
❑ 13	❑ 14	❑ 15
❑ 25	❑ 26	❑ 27
❑ 37	❑ 38	❑ 39
❑ 49	❑ 50	❑ 51
❑ 61	❑ 62	❑ 63
❑ 73	❑ 74	❑ 75
Total: ___	Total: ___	Total: ___
Rank: ___	Rank: ___	Rank: ___

COMPUTERS

- ❑ 4
- ❑ 16
- ❑ 28
- ❑ 40
- ❑ 52
- ❑ 64
- ❑ 76

Total: _____
Rank: _____

MATH

- ❑ 5
- ❑ 17
- ❑ 29
- ❑ 41
- ❑ 53
- ❑ 65
- ❑ 77

Total: _____
Rank: _____

MONEY

- ❑ 6
- ❑ 18
- ❑ 30
- ❑ 42
- ❑ 54
- ❑ 66
- ❑ 78

Total: _____
Rank: _____

MUSIC/DANCE

- ❑ 7
- ❑ 19
- ❑ 31
- ❑ 43
- ❑ 55
- ❑ 67
- ❑ 79

Total: _____
Rank: _____

SCIENCE

- ❑ 8
- ❑ 20
- ❑ 32
- ❑ 44
- ❑ 56
- ❑ 68
- ❑ 80

Total: _____
Rank: _____

SPORTS

- ❑ 9
- ❑ 21
- ❑ 33
- ❑ 45
- ❑ 57
- ❑ 69
- ❑ 81

Total: _____
Rank: _____

TALKING

- ❑ 10
- ❑ 22
- ❑ 34
- ❑ 46
- ❑ 58
- ❑ 70
- ❑ 82

Total: _____
Rank: _____

TRAVEL

- ❑ 11
- ❑ 23
- ❑ 35
- ❑ 47
- ❑ 59
- ❑ 71
- ❑ 83

Total: _____
Rank: _____

WRITING

- ❑ 12
- ❑ 24
- ❑ 36
- ❑ 48
- ❑ 60
- ❑ 72
- ❑ 84

Total: _____
Rank: _____

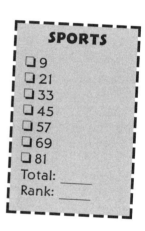

What are your top three interest areas? List them here (or on a separate piece of paper).

1. _____

2. _____

3. _____

WRITE YOUR RESPONSES ON A SEPARATE PIECE OF PAPER

This is your personal *Skill Set* and provides important clues about the kinds of work you're most likely to enjoy. Remember it and look for career ideas with a skill set that matches yours most closely.

TAKE A TRIP!

Cruise down the career idea highway and enjoy in-depth profiles of some of the interesting options in this field. Keep in mind all that you've discovered about yourself so far. Find the careers that match your own Skill Set first. After that, keep on trucking through the other ideas—exploration is the name of this game.

Ours is a world that's on the move. Whether on ground, by sea, or in the air, there are lots of opportunities for getting people where they want to go. Many people base an entire career on transportation, travel, or some aspect of the tourism and hospitality industry. Others, looking for some out-of-the-ordinary adventure, use it to launch or spice up a career. Then there are all the others for whom travel is just a part of getting the job done.

At any rate, travel is a common ingredient in a mind-boggling array of career options. From those who want to save the world to those who just want to see it, there's something for everyone.

The following chapters introduce an eclectic mix of ideas to consider. As you read through them, imagine yourself doing each job and ask yourself the following questions:

☀ Would I like it?
☀ Would I be good at it?
☀ Is it the stuff my career dreams are made of?

If so, make a quick exit to explore what it involves, try it out, check it out, and get acquainted!

Buckle up and enjoy the trip!

A NOTE ON WEBSITES

Internet sites tend to move around the Web a bit. If you have trouble finding a particular site, use an Internet browser to find a specific website or type of information.

Airline Personnel

SHORTCUTS

SKILL SET

✔ TRAVEL
✔ COMPUTERS
✔ ADVENTURE

GO to the airport and watch people at work. See if you can identify five different jobs.

READ *Opportunities in Airline Careers* by Adrian A. Paradis (Lincolnwood, Ill.: VGM Career Horizons, 1996).

TRY your hand at making the world's greatest paper airplane. Find ideas and inspiration in *Kids' Paper Airplane Book* by Ken Blackburn and Jeff Lammers (New York: Workman Publishing Company, 1996) or online at http://www.learn2.com/O6/O646/0646.asp.

WHAT ARE AIRLINE PERSONNEL?

Airline personnel include anybody and everybody who works at an airport. Starting with the parking attendants and baggage handlers who greet passengers as they arrive at the airport and ending with the pilots and flight attendants who get passengers where they need to go, there are many people who work to keep air travel safe and comfortable.

Pilots have the high-profile job of flying all kinds of sophisticated aircraft loaded with people and cargo. It takes a lot of skill and training to earn the trust of the thousands of people who board planes each day. The pilot's job begins an hour before the actual flight; two hours before if it is an international flight. This time is used to go over the flight plan, check weather conditions, brief the rest of the crew, and thoroughly check the airplane to make sure that everything is working properly. A commercial flight will usually have two pilots: a captain and a copilot who work in a cockpit filled with sophisticated computer systems and high-tech equipment. The captain is in charge and supervises the rest of the crew. The

captain and the copilot share the job of flying the plane. They work as a team especially during takeoff and landing, which are the most complicated parts of any flight.

Commercial airline pilots are required by the Federal Aviation Administration (FAA) to have an airline transport pilot's license. To qualify, a pilot has to be at least 23 years old and have at least 1,500 hours flying experience. They also have to pass a written FAA test as well as flight examinations. Major airlines like pilots to have some college; some even require a degree in an aviation-related field.

Some pilots enroll in a flight school or a university that has an aviation program. Over time, they build up the hours and different ratings necessary to fly for the major airlines. Others get the training and experience they need with the military.

Flight attendants are responsible for the safety and comfort of a flight's passengers. Like the pilots, their jobs begin about an hour before each flight. They are briefed about the flight by the captain and make sure that all the emergency equipment is in good working order and that the passenger cabin is in tip-top shape. They greet the passengers and help them find their seats. Before the plane takes off, the flight attendants go over all the safety features of the plane and let the passengers know what they need to do in case of an emergency.

During the flight, the attendants serve the passengers a snack or meal. However, the job requires much more than serving food and drinks to passengers. One of the most important parts of a flight attendant's job is never seen by most passengers. This responsibility involves doing whatever it takes to keep things on track during bad weather, medical emergencies, or other types of sky-high calamities.

Flight attendants are a cheerful bunch and have to be experts at dealing with people, even difficult ones. Passengers have more contact with flight attendants than with any other airline employees so they need to be customer service experts.

Flight attendants don't have to have a college degree but it doesn't hurt. Flight attendants should be very personable, poised, and professional. Some airlines have height and weight requirements. Flight attendants who are fluent in one or more foreign languages have a leg up on choice international flights. Airlines put new flight attendants through an intense training program that lasts several weeks.

Aircraft mechanics are the important folks who keep those big birds running safely. They fix things that aren't working properly and perform scheduled preventative maintenance in accordance with FAA guidelines. Aircraft mechanics work under a lot of pressure. A lot of lives depend on their getting the job done correctly and quickly. Most aircraft mechanics are trained at one of about 200 trade schools that are licensed by the FAA.

Although reservation agents don't see much of the passengers, they often provide passengers with that all-important first impression of the airline. That's because reservation agents are the people who provide flight information such as schedules, fares, and availability. By phone, they make flight reservations, assign seats, and take payments. Reservation agents usually have high school degrees. They need both computer and people skills. Specialized training can be obtained through any number of reputable travel schools or the airlines themselves.

Ticket agents manage the airline counter. They check-in passengers, process baggage, confirm or make seat assignments, and sell tickets. To qualify for this type of job, people need a high school degree, the ability to communicate well, and strong computer skills. Since they're the ones who deal with the fallout when a plane is delayed or rerouted, a healthy dose of patience is often useful when dealing with irritated, and sometimes irate, customers.

Pilots and flight attendants have the most high-profile jobs, and they obviously do the most traveling. Other airline employees don't travel as part of their jobs, but they do receive flight benefits that allow them to fly for free or at dramatically reduced prices.

Airline employees should be prepared to live near a major airline hub such as Dallas, New York, Atlanta, Los Angeles, or Chicago. Since airlines run 24 hours a day, seven days a week, all airline employees can expect to work some crazy hours—especially during the holidays or other peak flying times.

It's hard to get a feel for an entire industry in one short chapter, especially one that involves so many interesting career options. If you're really interested in working for an airline someday, take off and do some research on your own. You'll find chapters on what it's like to be an aircraft controller or flight attendant in *Career Ideas for Kids Who Like Talking* and one on pilots in *Career Ideas for Kids Who Like Adventure.*

TRY IT OUT!

UP, UP, AND AWAY
Step into the cockpit with Microsoft Flight Simulator. Choose your aircraft, create your flight plan, check your instruments, and take off. You'll have to deal with weather conditions and potential disaster just like a real pilot. Flight Simulator has a huge following and the official website at http://www. microsoft.com/games/fs2000/features.asp even has a plan that will help you fly around the world.

PEOPLE WHO NEED PEOPLE

Get involved in an activity that will help you develop the people skills you'll need for an airline job. A local hospital might be a good place to start. Volunteer to work as a "candy striper." Candy stripers have lots of contact with patients. They deliver flowers, push the juice cart, and visit patients.

Hospitals aren't the only places that need volunteers to work with people. Check out nursing homes and soup kitchens. Maybe a nearby child-care center or library could use your help reading stories to younger children. Your local United Way or Junior League are organizations that sponsor volunteer projects where you can practice your people skills and do some good at the same time. Check your local telephone directory for phone numbers for various types of volunteer organizations.

ADVANCE RESERVATIONS

Get some practice being a reservation agent with Delta's website at http://www.delta.com. Use their on-line reservation system to check out fares between different locations. Enter different places, times, and dates. Make note of how the day, the time, and the amount of advanced notice you give effects the fare. Try to find the best deal. Also, check and see how much extra it costs to fly first class.

ON-LINE TRAVEL

While you're on-line, check out some of these interesting airline sites.

- ☿ Get the scoop on these and other airline jobs at http://www.jobmonkey.com/airline/index.html.
- ☿ Visit the FAA's site at http://www.faa.gov.
- ☿ Flight Attendant's Resource Center at http://www.flightattendants.org.
- ☿ Another site for flight attendants is In-Flight at http://www.inflight.bizland.com.
- ☿ FlightAttendants.org at http://www.flightattendants.org is a site for flight attendants past, present, and future.

☼ Get an objective view of flight aviation safety developments at the Flight Safety Foundation's site at http://www.flightsafety.org.

☼ Check out JetCareers for some good information about how to become a pilot at http://www.jetcareers.com.

☼ Find some cool aviation links at http://www.flightinfo. com/html/cool_links.shtm.

☼ Take an aviation trivia challenge at http://www.flightinfo. com/cgi-bin.

☼ Locate an aviation school near you at http://www. flightinfo.com/html/schools.shtm.

☼ Look at Delta's requirements for pilots at http://www. dalpa.com/public/requirements.htm.

BOOK A FLIGHT

Delve into the different careers in the airline industry by checking out some of these books.

Bock, Becky S., and Cheryl A. Cage. *Welcome Aboard! Your Career as a Flight Attendant.* Englewood, Colo.: Cage Consulting, Inc., 1998.

Griffin, Jeff. *Becoming an Airline Pilot.* New York: Tab Books, 1990.

Kirkwood, Tim. *Flight Attendant Job Finder & Career Guide.* River Forest, Ill.: Planning Communications, 1999.

March, Carol. *Choosing an Airline Career: In-Depth Descriptions of Entry-Level Positions, Travel Benefits, How to Apply and Interview.* Denver: Capri Publishing, 1993.

Mark, Robert P. *Professional Pilot Career Guide.* New York: McGraw-Hill Professional Publishing, 1999.

Otypka, Sylvia J. *Flying the Big Birds: On Becoming an Airline Pilot.* Oak Brook, Ill.: Leading Edge Publishing, 1998.

Paradis, Adrian A. *Opportunities in Airline Careers.* Lincolnwood, Ill.: VGM Career Horizons, 1996.

Taver, Judy A. *Flight Plan to the Flight Deck: Strategies for a Pilot Career.* Englewood, Colo.: Cage Consulting, Inc., 1997.

Ward, Kiki. *The Essential Guide to Becoming a Flight Attendant.* Colleyville, Tex.: Kiwi Productions, 2000.

CHECK IT OUT

Airline Dispatchers Federation
700 13th Street NW, Suite 950
Washington, D.C. 20005
http://www.dispatch.org

Airline Employees International
5600 S. Central Avenue
Chicago, Illinois 60638

Airline Pilots Association
1625 Massachusetts Avenue NW
Washington, D.C. 20036
http://www.alpa.org/

Air Transport Association of
America
1301 Pennsylvania Avenue NW
Washington, D.C. 20006
http://www.air-transport.org/

Association of Flight Attendants
1275 K Street NW
Washington, D.C. 20005-4006
http://www.afanet.org/

International Federation of
Flight Attendants
630 Third Avenue, 5th Floor
New York, New York 10017

Professional Aviation
Maintenance Association
636 I Street NW, Suite 300
Washington, D.C. 20001
http://www.pama.org

GET ACQUAINTED

Jon Goodman,
Airline Personnel

CAREER PATH

CHILDHOOD ASPIRATION: To be a pilot.

FIRST JOB: Bag boy at a local grocery store.

CURRENT JOB: Manager of flight control for Midway Airlines.

UP, UP, AND AWAY

Jon Goodman has never been able to resist looking up when-ever an airplane flies overhead. For as far back as he can remember, Goodman always wanted to be a pilot.

When high school graduation rolled around, Goodman was-n't like a lot of his friends who all seemed to be heading off to the same colleges for degrees in business administration. He knew that somehow, some way he wanted planes in his future, so he started checking out some career options in avi-ation. What he discovered was Embry-Riddle Aeronautical University, a great aviation school in Daytona Beach, Florida.

Money—that is, the lack thereof—stood in the way of Goodman just dropping everything and heading to Florida to enroll. Also, he had married just one year out of high school, so his decisions affected his wife as well. Not to be deterred for long, Goodman set about working for a couple years to save enough money for tuition. All along, he took basic courses at a nearby community college that would transfer into the aviation program when he got there.

It might not have been the most direct route to get a col-lege degree, but it worked. While at Embry-Riddle, Goodman learned how to be a pilot and earned both his private and commercial pilot licenses. On the advice of his golf coach, Goodman also earned an airline dispatcher credential. That way he was prepared for a career in the air or on the ground.

BREAK A LEG!

Goodman fully expected to become a military pilot as soon as he graduated from college. He had even completed half of his training as a marine officer before he injured his leg and wound up on crutches. Yes, he could have gone back for another whirl at the training after his leg healed, but with both his school loans coming due and a second baby on the way, Goodman needed a sure thing—right now!

That's when he got a job as a "flight follower" for a small commuter airline. Although his main job was on the ground, he often got the chance to fly mechanics back and forth between the airport and the airline's maintenance center. In one way, it was the best of both worlds: Goodman got to fly, but he also got to learn more about the operations side of the airline business.

THE RIGHT PLACE AT THE RIGHT TIME

Next on the career path was an opportunity to join a new airline as one of its first four dispatchers. It meant a move to Chicago, but it turned out to be a good move. Midway, Goodman's new employer, grew quickly and so did Goodman's career. He moved up to the role of flight dispatch coordinator and is now the manager of the entire flight dispatch operations center.

Goodman's team of 20 dispatchers is responsible for 34 airplanes, which fly a total of 200 flights per day to 25 different cities. Midway is a "hub and spoke" operation, meaning that every flight leaves and returns to the airline's hub in Raleigh, North Carolina. This mode of operation makes it especially important that all flights remain as close to on time as possible. One delayed flight can cause many other flights to be delayed as well. After all, it is the airline's business to make certain all passengers, including connecting passengers, get to their final destination. But, while schedule integrity (keeping flights on time) is Goodman's number-two goal, the number-one goal is safety.

Goodman describes the work of a flight dispatcher as being "a pilot on the ground." According to federal regulations, the dispatcher is responsible, along with the captain, for the operational control, planning, and safety of each flight. In fact, no airplanes are authorized to leave the ground without clearance from a flight dispatcher. Dispatchers plan and monitor the flights, and they analyze weather conditions and mechanical airworthiness using a variety of systems available including phone consultations and Internet resources. If dispatch says no, the planes don't go!

Chief Purser

SKILL SET

✔ TRAVEL

✔ TALKING

✔ MATH

WHAT IS A CHIEF PURSER?

Cruise ships travel to many exotic places including the Mediterranean, Alaska, and the Caribbean Islands. One of the top-ranking officers aboard a cruise ship is the chief purser.

Think of a cruise ship as a very large floating resort and the purser's office as the front desk. Pursers handle the ship's business dealings, which put them in contact with lots of paperwork and lots of people. Passengers rely on pursers for exchanging currency, cashing checks, mailing letters, or renting safe-deposit boxes. The purser's office also handles any cabin changes or upgrades.

The ship's crew relies on pursers to handle all the human resources duties, such as payroll, scheduling, and crew accommodations. The purser's office is responsible for essentially anything that has to do with money: passenger accounts, casino receipts, and budget management as well as various accounting and auditing tasks.

Another important function of the purser's office involves handling immigration and customs matters. Special documents are required every time the ship enters or leaves a port, and it's the purser's job to make sure this paperwork is done correctly.

The chief purser has the top job in the purser's office and works with a staff of assistants to cover all the bases. Some matters are handled by the chief purser, while others are delegated to a staff that includes first, second, and third pursers, and the crew purser.

While pursers gain experience and rise through the ranks, they are likely to have seen the world at least a few times over and have earned some fairly attractive perks along the way. Food, lodging, and travel are part of the job, and chief pursers are usually given a private cabin, which is not the case for most cruise ship employees. The cruise line will pay your airfare to and from the port from which you are sailing. The pay is not bad considering that pursers have virtually no expenses while at sea. The cruise line even provides clean uniforms to wear on the job!

Of course, life as a purser is not all fun and games. Days at sea can be long, and days off are few. As with all jobs, it helps to weigh the pros and cons before deciding to be a purser.

Certain skills, such as good people skills, seem to serve chief pursers well. That's because people play such a big part in the job. In a given day, pursers have contact with passengers, staff members, fellow crewmates, and foreign government officials. Accounting skills are helpful in handling the money matters related to the job, and management skills are useful in keeping the multiple responsibilities on track.

Chief pursers have backgrounds and training similar to hotel managers. Many receive a degree in hotel management and may work in other areas of hospitality before landing a chief purser's job. Others gradually work their way through the ranks of the purser's office.

Chief pursers, like most other cruise ship staff, work on a contract basis. Most contracts are from four to six months long. Those who do a good job are offered another contract. Those who don't will need to look elsewhere.

TRY IT OUT

PURSER FOR HIRE

If you were in the market for a job as a purser, the Internet would be a great place to find one. Here are some websites that offer information about the job duties, pay, and benefits currently offered in this line of work.

- http://www.overseasjobs.com/do/details/35236
- http://www.coolworks.com
- http://www.cruiseshipjob.com/personne.htm
- http://www.hcareers.com

GET A HEAD START

There's no time like the present to start gaining the valuable math and customer service experience you'll need to be a chief purser. Check with your school to see if you can find some activities that will help you gain both. For example, working the concession stand at a school sporting event will get you used to handling money and dealing with people. Also, don't forget to enroll in some business accounting classes.

TAKE A QUIZ

Find out how cruise-ship savvy you are by playing the "Are You Ship Shape?" trivia game at http://www.shipcenter. com/quiz.

CYBER CRUISING

While you are on-line, visit some of these cruise-related sites.

☀ Start with some of the major cruise line sites:
Carnival Cruises at http://www.carnival.com.
Holland America at http://www.hollandamerica.com.
Disney Cruise Line at http://disney.go.com/
DisneyCruise/index.html.
Princess Cruise Line at http://www.princesscruises.com.
Norwegian Cruise Line at http://www.ncl.com.
☀ Check out TravelPage's CruisePage at http://www. cruiseserver.net/travelpage for cruise news, cruise deals, ship profiles, and cruise links.
☀ Visit CruiseTrade, the business paper of the cruise industry on-line at http://www.traveltrade.com/ cruisetrade/index.shtml.
☀ Find a huge listing of cruise related links at http://www.ucs.mun.ca/~rklein/cruise.html.
☀ Learn about working on cruise ships at http://www.exbyte.com/cruise/cruise.htm.
☀ Discover the "real truth" about cruise ship jobs at http://www.shipjobs.com.
☀ The National Career Networking Association has a thorough section on cruise ship employment at http://ncna.com/cruise.html.

SEASIDE READING

Set sail for the library and check out some of these books about cruise-ship careers.

Bow, Sandra. *Working on Cruise Ships.* Cincinnati, Ohio: Seven Hills Book Distribution, 1999.

Eberts, Marjorie, Linda Brothers, and Ann Gisler. *Careers in Travel, Tourism and Hospitality.* Lincolnwood, Ill.: NTC Publishing Group, 1997.

Hawks, John K. *Travel and Tourism: A Comprehensive Guide to the Exciting Careers Open to You in the Travel and Tourism Industry.* New York: Facts On File, 1996.

Heath, Andy. *Cruising for a Living: How to Find Your Dream Job on a Luxury Cruise Ship.* Toronto, Ontario: INFACT Publishing, 1995.

Kennedy, Don H. *How to Get a Job on a Cruise Ship.* Atlanta: CareerSource Publications, 2000.

Maltzman, Jeffrey. *Jobs in Paradise: The Definitive Guide to Exotic Jobs Everywhere.* New York: HarperPerennial Library, 1993.

Miller, Mary Fallon. *How to Get a Job with a Cruise Line: How to Sail Around the World on Luxury Cruise Ships and Get Paid for It.* St. Petersburg, Fla.: Ticket to Adventure, 1997.

CHECK IT OUT

Cruise Line International Association
500 Fifth Avenue, Suite 1407
New York, New York 10010
http://www.cruising.org

International Council of Cruise Lines
2111 Wilson Boulevard, 8th Floor
Arlington, Virginia 22201
http://www.iccl.org

North West Cruiseship Association
1111 W. Hastings Street
Vancouver, British Columbia V6E213
http://www.alaskacruises.org

Shipbuilders Council of America
1600 Wilson Boulevard, Suite 1000
Arlington, Virginia 22209
http://www.shipbuilders.org

GET ACQUAINTED

Bernard Hamburger,
Chief Purser

CAREER PATH

CHILDHOOD ASPIRATION:
Doesn't recall a fixed job idea but
considered everything from pilot
to politician.

FIRST JOB: Stock boy in a
grocery store.

CURRENT JOB: Purser for
Holland America Line.

Hamburger with his wife
and daughters, his favorite
travel companions.

NOTHING TO LOSE

Bernard Hamburger grew up in Holland where he studied for
four years to be a scientific librarian. After he graduated from
college, he got a job as a librarian but lasted only six weeks.
He discovered that, much as he loved the subject of library
science, working as a librarian just didn't cut it—there wasn't
enough happening.

With nothing to lose, he applied for a job leading tours in
Italy, Greece, and Kenya. He had no experience as a tour
guide, but he happened to be fluent in five different languages—Dutch, English, German, French, and Italian—and
was hired on the spot. Hamburger credits geography for his
language skills. Holland is surrounded by different countries,
all of which speak different languages. Getting along with the
neighbors takes on a whole new meaning in a situation like
that!

BON VOYAGE!

When Hamburger decided it was time to move on to something else, his brother-in-law, an engineer for Holland

America, suggested that he apply for a job with the cruise line's hotel department. Listing his language experience, his travel experience, and his college degree on the application, Hamburger was a shoo-in for the job; he was hired as a management trainee and eventually became a purser.

Several years into his career, Hamburger has circled the globe and visited some 90 countries on every continent in the world. From St. Petersburg to Alexandria, Monte Carlo to Bora Bora, Hamburger has seen them all and loved every minute of it. His all-time favorite port is Quebec, a city he describes as "great." New York and Monte Carlo tie for second favorites.

While at sea, Hamburger manages all the financial affairs of the ship. He oversees the payroll process as well as book-keeping and revenue reporting. Much of his workday is spent behind a desk working on a computer. When in port, Hamburger's job is to clear the ship with local authorities so that everyone can disembark and do some sightseeing. Twice a week Hamburger, along with the ship's other officers, gets dressed up in full uniform for formal dinner parties with the guests.

WHAT A LIFE!

Hamburger has found that working at sea is more of a lifestyle than a job. His wife and two young children travel with him. They spend four or five months at sea followed by two months spent doing whatever they like. Even though he works seven days a week when on board the ship, his hours are flexible. He can come in as early as he wants or work as late as he wants. When the ship is in port, he finds time to see the sights with his family by working extra hours during the days before and after.

It's an unusual way of life but one that works well for his family. His children have already seen more of the world than most people see in a lifetime. The family enjoys a rich, full life together that puts a new spin on "quality" time. Playing on the world's most pristine beaches, enjoying the sights and sounds of the world's most interesting places, meeting peo-

ple from every conceivable culture and background—now that's quality time.

The best part of all? No commuting! Hamburger lives where he works so he doesn't get caught up in the rat race of traffic jams and the other rigamarole associated with more traditional corporate jobs.

EDUCATION PAYS OFF

Hamburger says that he wouldn't be where he is today without that degree in library science, even though it has little to do with what he is doing. As Hamburger says, education opens doors, or in his case, hatches.

TAKE A TRIP!

Commercial Fisher

SKILL SET

✔ **ANIMALS & NATURE**

✔ **TRAVEL**

✔ **ADVENTURE**

SHORTCUTS

GO fishing!

READ *Eyewitness: Fish* by Steve Parker and Dave King (New York: DK Publishing, 2000).

TRY going online to http://www.nmfs.noaa.gov where you'll find all kids of "fishy" information. There's even a special kid's corner!

WHAT IS A COMMERCIAL FISHER?

Gone fishing! It's the rallying cry of weekend fishers everywhere. But grabbing a fishing pole and some worms isn't what commercial fishing is about. Commercial fishers bring in tons of fish each year—sometimes braving rough seas and harsh weather to satisfy the world's seafood lovers.

It takes several things to be a commercial fisher: First, of course, fishers need access to lots of water and plenty of fish. That's why many fishers tend to live near oceans. But finding fish isn't always easy. Fishers have to know a lot about the habits of fish—where they travel and when. And fishers also have to follow specific government regulations as they try to make a living.

Weather is another contributing factor to a fisher's livelihood. Although there's not a thing anyone can do about it, weather often makes the difference between a successful year of fishing and a complete washout. Even in the best of circumstances, commercial fishers encounter bouts of nasty weather that make the job all the more challenging. Weather also guides fishing patterns and locations. For instance, herring spawn might be the "catch of the day" during the winter months, while halibut are plentiful in the spring. Some fishers work only during the summer or winter months. Others work year-round, although that sometimes means

36

going to where the fish are at different times of the year—maybe it's Alaska in the summer and Seattle during the winter.

Water, fish, and weather cover the basic "tools" of the trade, but there are two other important factors. One is the boat and the other is people to buy the fish. The first is sometimes harder to come by than the second. That's because boats are very expensive to buy and maintain, which is why most commercial fishers don't own their own boats but instead work for companies or other people who do.

As for people to buy the fish, that's a whole industry in and of itself. Fishers generally make an arrangement with one or more seafood processing plants that bring their catch to market. In some places in the world, fish is a daily part of people's diets. In America, some types of fish are considered a delicacy, while others, like tuna and salmon, are more common.

In the United States, Alaska is the fishing "hot spot." According to the National Marine Fisheries Service, there are about 16,400 registered fishing vessels in that state and as many as 50,000 to 60,000 people working in Alaska's

commercial fishing industry (although not all of these people actually catch fish).

As for training, more often than not commercial fishing is a trade that's learned on the job. Like farming and other types of strenuous, outdoor occupations, fishing is one of those careers that some people thrive on. In some fishing towns, it is not uncommon for fishing to go back several generations in certain families. Women as well as men are found on commercial fishing vessels everywhere. Fishing is certainly an equal opportunity employer. Any good fisher needs the stamina to work long hours, a respect for the wily ways of nature, and a willingness to work hard.

Those people interested in the more scientific and technical aspects of the fishing industry might choose to pursue a college degree in fisheries science or commercial fish harvesting. Another option is to learn about vessel operations through a program that specializes in maritime studies, or to get safety training by joining the U.S. Coast Guard.

TRY IT OUT

GO FISH!

You may not have access to a commercial fishing vessel or even one of those charter fishing boats so popular in many tourist areas, but you can start your fishing career with just a rod and a good-sized pond or lake. Ask a parent or trusted adult to take you fishing, and see what you think. If it's your first time out for a good catch, go on-line for some fishing tips at http://www.family.com and search for "a beginner's guide to fishing."

No fishing expedition is complete without cleaning the fish and enjoying a fresh fish dinner!

FISHING FOR FUN

While the educational value of some of the following websites may be questionable, they'll provide a few minutes of fun as you learn more about sea life and fishing.

✵ Biggest, Smallest, Fastest, Deepest: Marine Animal Records at http://www.oceanlink.island.net/records.html
✵ Fishin' for Facts Library at http://www.whaletimes.org/whafshn.htm
✵ Gone Fishin' Crossword Puzzle at http://www.spav.com/sa/sakids/games/crossword/default.html
✵ Guppy Races at http://www.cruzio.com/~sabweb/sabfx/guppy.html
✵ Online Knots at http://www.spav.com/sa/sakids/coolstuff/knots/fishermans/default.html

FISHING FOR BOOKS

Here are some books that provide information about sea life.

Baker, Lucy. *Life in the Oceans.* New York: Scholastic, 1993.

Ganeri, Anita. *The Oceans Atlas.* New York: Dorling Kindersley, 1995.

Klein, John F., and Carol Gaskin. *A Day in the Life of a Commercial Fisherman.* Mahwah. N.J.: Troll Associates, 1988.

Koch, Frances King. *Mariculture: Farming the Fruits of the Sea.* Danbury, Conn.: Franklin Watts, 1992.

Rogers, Daniel. *Food From the Sea.* Danbury, Conn.: Franklin Watts, 1991.

VanCleave, Janice. *Oceans for Every Kid.* New York: John Wiley & Sons, 1996.

Wells, Susan. *The Illustrated World of Oceans.* New York: Simon and Schuster, 1993.

Zim, Herbert, and Hurst Shoemaker. *Fishes.* North Platte, Nebr.: Western Publishing Company, 1987.

FISHING FOR EMPLOYMENT

To get a look at all the different jobs available in the fishing industry, visit these two websites:

✵ Seafood Industry Jobs Network at http://www.fishjobs.com

🔆 Commercial Fishing Industry at http://www.
maritimejobs.net

Take note of the skills required for each type of job, the salary, the locations of various jobs, and compare what you think are the best opportunities.

KA-CHING!

Follow the money and find out the going rate for fish today. Go on-line to Fishery Market News at http://www.st. nmfs.gov/st1/market_news/index.html and compare how much Boston fishers are getting for lobster with what Gulf fishers are getting for shrimp. This website includes up-to-date prices of everything from clams to whiting. If a pound of lobster goes for $3.40, how much would you get for a ton?

CHECK IT OUT

American Fisheries Society
5410 Grosvenor Lane,
   Suite 110
Bethesda, Maryland 20814
http://www.fisheries.org

American Fisherman's
   Research Foundation
P.O. Box 138
Eureka, California 95502
http://www.afrf.org

Deep Sea Fisherman's Union
5215 Ballard Avenue NW
Seattle, Washington 98107
http://www.dsfu.org

Fishermen's Marketing
   Association
320 2nd Street, Suite 2B
Eureka, California 95501
http://www.trawl.org

National Fisheries Institute
1901 N. Fort Myers Drive,
   Suite 700
Arlington, Virginia 22209
http://www.nfi.org

Women's Fisheries Network
P.O. Box 1432 GMF
Boston, Massachusetts 02205
http://web.mit.edu/org/s/
   seagrant/www/wfn.html

GET ACQUAINTED

Kirby Green,
Commercial Fisher

CAREER PATH

CHILDHOOD ASPIRATION: To be a fisherman.

FIRST JOB: Working on his dad's boat one summer in exchange for a BMX bike.

CURRENT JOB: Commercial fisherman.

LIKE FATHER, LIKE SON

Kirby Green was born on a small fishing island in Alaska where his father was a fisherman. He and his family lived there, miserable winters and all, until his mother put her foot down and insisted that they move somewhere with a more comfortable climate. Hawaii seemed to fit the bill, so the family moved there when Green was eight. His father spent the summers fishing in Alaska and would often let Green tag along.

Green loved fishing, but once he graduated from high school, he thought he should give something else a try—just to be sure fishing was what he really wanted to do with his life. He decided that teaching might be a good thing for him to consider. He spent two years in college and then returned to his first love—the ocean.

It took some scrimping and saving and lots of hard work, but by the time Green was 21 years old, he'd managed to get enough cash together to put a down payment on his own boat. The *Janet G* is his pride and joy. Built in 1929 and 56 feet long, the boat holds 50,000 pounds of fish.

FISHER'S HOURS

Green and his crew fish in Alaskan waters from June through September. On a good day, the crew can fill *Janet G* in a couple of hours; other times it takes a couple of days. Either way, these months are filled with long hours and hard work.

This schedule gives Green several months off to knock around and do other things from his home base in Seattle. Travel consumes as much free time as Green's schedule and budget will allow. Otherwise, the time is filled working on the *Janet G,* working out at the gym, and doing repairs for other businesses around town.

A BAD FISH DAY

It's a bad day when you go out on your beat and don't catch enough fish to pay the costs of fuel and broken equipment. And it's a bad day or when the weather gets crazy, and you have to struggle to stay afloat. Some days are like that, but most of them aren't.

As with most jobs, fishing has both good and bad points. On Green's list, the pros far outweigh the cons. Of course, the job gets dangerous at times, and you can get tired of working with the same four or five people all day. However, working outdoors and enjoying some of the most amazing scenery in the world is a cool way to make a living. Green says it's pretty exciting on those days when you set your nets once and end up with 30,000 to 40,000 pounds of fish. It can also be fun just to goof off on board the ship or just to relax and let your mind wander. Those things you can't very well do in a typical office environment.

Green admits that fishing is one of those careers that you either love or hate. Lucky for Green, fishing is it for him!

P.S.

For more details about Green's life as a commercial fisher, visit his website at http://www.janetg.com.

Cruise Director

SHORTCUTS

GO to a travel agency and get some cruise line brochures. Check out the different kinds of activities each offers.

READ the on-line version of *National Geographic Traveler* at http:www.national-geographic.com/traveler.

TRY taking a course in public speaking.

WHAT IS A CRUISE DIRECTOR?

Cruising on a luxurious ship to exotic places all over the world is a dream vacation for all kinds of people—newlyweds enjoying their honeymoons, families creating memories, older folks making the most of their retirement years, and young singles looking for fun. No matter why they set sail, taking a cruise is expensive, and people come aboard expecting to get their money's worth. It's the cruise director's job to make sure that all passengers enjoy their experiences.

Think of a cruise ship as a luxurious resort that floats. These ships have all the amenities of the grandest hotel and more. A cruise ship has wonderful accommodations, incredible food, and nonstop activities—and that's just the beginning. Add lots of pools and outdoor sports, at least one theater, a health club, and several nightclubs, and you've got the makings of quite a vacation. Daily entertainment might include a Broadway-type stage show, line dancing with a DJ, a formal gala, a comedy show, a magic show, karaoke, and several different styles of bands.

Still looking for something to do? How about some fun and games such as bingo, scavenger hunts, talent shows, and trivia contests? Then, of course, there are exciting days to be spent in port with plenty of shopping and sightseeing for all.

So what does a cruise director have to do with all this? Everything! A cruise director is responsible for all the planning, scheduling, and hiring it takes to keep things hoppin' on board a cruise ship. Fortunately, cruise directors don't have to do all the work themselves. Instead, they manage a fairly large staff of assistants and entertainers.

A cruise director's job starts long before the first passenger boards the ship. All of the activities have to be dreamed up, thoroughly planned, staffed, and scheduled. Entertainment options must offer something for everyone, from swinging singles to senior citizens and everyone in between. This means planning some "generic" activities that appeal to all as well as some specific to the different groups represented on the ship.

Once the planning is done and the ship sets sail, the real work begins! A daily schedule of events is distributed to passengers every day. With a variety of activities running nearly 24 hours a day, it's not hard to imagine the many hours a cruise director works while at sea.

Cruise directors often set the tone for an entire cruise. Their high-profile duties run the gamut from calling bingo games, and warming up audiences for special performances to hosting cocktail parties. A winning personality and great people skills are at the top of the list of required job skills. Cruise directors must be cool, calm, and collected as they respond to situations that would send most people into a tailspin. Grumpy customers? Smile and deal with it. Four days of bad weather with no end in sight? Smile and make the most of it. A major act in the entertainment lineup cancels at the last minute? Smile and make sure the show goes on without a hitch.

It's a big job and one that's not for everyone. But the job does come with some very attractive perks. Traveling to all kinds of exciting places tops the list. Then there's the fact that cruise directors tend to be paid pretty well. They also have their own cabins on the ship and eat the same great food that the passengers pay big bucks to enjoy.

A college degree is not required to become a cruise director, but a degree in public relations or hospitality certainly looks good on a resume and often gives a needed edge over other applicants. Proficiency in a foreign language is also helpful as is lots of public speaking experience.

Of course, no one gets a job as a cruise director without putting in some time in other areas of the ship. It's called paying your dues, and it's all part of getting the experience needed to handle all the responsibilities assigned to a cruise director. Many cruise directors start out as entertainers or youth counselors on board and work their way up to assistant cruise director. Landing the plum job as cruise director can take several years.

TRY IT OUT

VIRTUAL CRUISE DIRECTOR

Try your hand at planning a day's events for an imaginary cruise ship. Get an idea of what kind of activities are common by looking at a typical day on a Princess cruise at http://www.grandprincess.com/onboard/activities.html. Get some ideas for production shows at http://www.cruise-eta.com.

Then, find some entertainers at http://www.grandprincess. com/onboard/entertain.html and http://www.leepentertainment.com/specialtyacts.html.

Make sure your plans include ideas that appeal to kids your own age, someone your parents' age, and even people your grandparents' age. Make a poster listing the day's events in an easy-to-read and very classy format.

A FAMILY AFFAIR

Plan some activities for your next family get-together. Think of some games that everyone will enjoy. Charades, anyone? Also, plan some specific activities for children, teenagers, moms and dads, and the older folks. Get some planning tips on-line at http://www.learn2.com/06/0662/0662.asp and http://www.family-reunion.com.

A JUGGLING ACT

Does your school or place of worship put on a talent show, a carnival, or fall festival? Get involved by volunteering to help out in any way you can.

Make sure to take note of the different types of activities offered at each event. Which ones have the little kids begging for more? Which ones get the adults smiling?

ON-LINE CRUISING

You can learn a lot about the cruise ship industry on-line. Start by visiting some of the major cruise line sites such as:

- Carnival Cruises at http://www.carnival.com.
- Holland America at http://www.hollandamerica.com.
- Disney Cruise Line at http://disney.go.com/DisneyCruise/index.html.
- Princess Cruise Line at http://www. princesscruises.com.
- Norwegian Cruise Line at http://www.ncl.com.

For more cruise-related information, visit some of these websites as well:

☼ Check out TravelPage's CruisePage at http://www. cruiseserver.net/travelpage for cruise news, cruise deals, ship profiles, and cruise links.

☼ Visit Cruise Trade, the business paper of the cruise industry on-line at http://www.traveltrade.com/ cruisetrade/index.shtml.

☼ Find a huge listing of cruise-related links at http://www.ucs.mum.ca/~rklein/cruise.html.

☼ Learn about working on cruise ships at http://www.exbyte.com/cruise/cruise.htm.

☼ Discover the "real truth" about cruise ship jobs at http://www.shipjobs.com.

☼ The National Career Networking Association has a thorough section on cruise ship employment at http://ncna.com/cruise.html.

☼ Read an interview with a very experienced cruise director at http://www.cruises.about.com/travel/ cruises/library/weekly/aa083099.htm.

THE INSIDE SCOOP

Set sail for the library and check out some of these books on cruise ship careers.

———————————

Bow, Sandra. *Working on Cruise Ships.* Cincinnati, Ohio: Seven Hills Book Distribution, 1999.

Eberts, Marjorie, Linda Brothers, and Ann Gisler. *Careers in Travel, Tourism and Hospitality.* Lincolnwood, Ill.: NTC Publishing Group, 1997.

Heath, Andy. *Cruising for a Living: How to Find Your Dream Job on a Luxury Cruise Ship.* Toronto: INFACT Publishing, 1995.

Kennedy, Don H. *Exploring Careers on Cruise Ships.* New York: Rosen Publishing Group, 1993.

———. *How to Get a Job on a Cruise Ship.* Atlanta, Ga.: CareerSource Publications, 2000.

Miller, Mary Fallon. *How to Get a Job with a Cruise Line: How to Sail Around the World on Luxury Cruise Ships and Get Paid for It.* St. Petersburg, Fla.: Ticket to Adventure, 1997.

———————————

CHECK IT OUT

Cruise Lines International Association
500 Fifth Avenue, Suite 1407
New York, New York 10010
http://www.cruising.org

International Council of Cruise Lines
2111 Wilson Boulevard, 8th Floor
Arlington, Virginia 22201
http://www.iccl.org

North West Cruiseship Association
1111 W. Hastings Street
Vancouver, British Columbia V6E213
http://www.alaskacruises.org

Shipbuilders Council of America
1600 Wilson Boulevard, Suite 1000
Arlington, Virginia 22209
http://www.shipbuilders.org

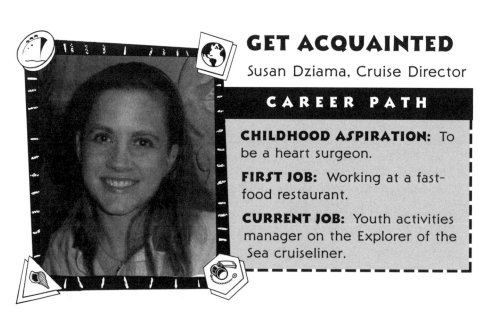

GET ACQUAINTED

Susan Dziama, Cruise Director

CAREER PATH

CHILDHOOD ASPIRATION: To be a heart surgeon.

FIRST JOB: Working at a fast-food restaurant.

CURRENT JOB: Youth activities manager on the Explorer of the Sea cruiseliner.

HEARTFELT AMBITIONS

When Susan Dziama first starting thinking about her future career, she put her desire to help people together with her interest in science. That led to the idea of becoming a heart surgeon. When she went to college, she even minored in biology, which is a good pre-med choice.

Her major was secondary education with an emphasis in physical education. And that major turned out to be a great fit for the job she landed just one week after she graduated. No, it wasn't a job as a heart surgeon. It wasn't even a job as a high school physical education teacher.

It was a job that Dziama applied for after seeing a sign on campus advertising for summer work on a cruise line. Since Dziama graduated in May and schoolteachers typically don't start teaching until August or September, she had an empty summer looming ahead and decided to fill it with some adventure. After a couple rounds of interviews, Dziama was offered a job managing youth activities aboard a Royal Caribbean cruise ship. Talk about perfect timing! The offer came in one day before she graduated. Within a week, all her belongings were safely stowed at her parents' house, and she was on her way to New York for training.

YOU MEAN I GET PAID FOR THIS?

Dziama's job is cruise director for the younger set. She and her staff of 14 entertain between 100 and 800 children and teens every week for five months straight. Their days begin at 9:00 A.M. and end at 2:00 A.M. (yes, that's A.M.!). Activities are planned for four different age groups—the little folks who are three to five, the kids who are six to eight, the big kids who are nine to 12, and the 13- to 17-year-old teens. The daily schedule is jam-packed with what Dziama calls "camp at sea." There are adventures in science, computer art projects, theme nights, dinner at the Johnny Rocket Diner, and dancing and entertainment at the teen nightclub (that's where the late nights come in).

It's all done with one goal in mind—everybody's got to have fun! Little did Dziama realize when she signed her first contract that she'd be having as much fun as the kids. She says paydays are just icing on the cake.

HOME SWEET BERTH

Dziama is a manager, so she gets her own cabin on board the ship where she lives for 10 months out of the year. She says it's like living on a floating city. The crew has there own mess hall, nightclub, gym, and activities manager—all the comforts of home at sea.

Every year, Dziama gets two months of vacation time. She generally spends a couple weeks visiting her family and the rest gallivanting to new places she wants to explore. So far, these travels have included London, Paris, and San Francisco.

SETTING SAIL

Dziama's first assignment was aboard the cruise ship *Voyager*, which regularly set sail for such exotic ports as Haiti, Jamaica, Panama, and Bermuda. She was recently reassigned to the brand-new *Explorer*, which docks in Miami en route to hot spots such as San Juan, St. Thomas, and Nassau. What a life!

Diplomat

SHORTCUTS

SKILL SET

✔ TRAVEL
✔ WRITING
✔ TALKING

GO to United Nations on-line at http://www.unol.org/info.shtml.

READ *Inside a U.S. Embassy: How the Foreign Service Works for America* on-line at http://www.afsa.org/inside/index.html.

TRY taking lots of writing, public speaking, and foreign language courses.

WHAT IS A DIPLOMAT?

Choose to pursue a career as a diplomat and you choose much more than a job; it's a way of life that often requires commitment, dedication, and personal sacrifice. A diplomat represents the United States and promotes its values and interests around the world—whenever and wherever they are needed.

Diplomats, or foreign service officers, as they are also called, work at the State Department in Washington, D.C., and in embassies and consulates in almost every recognized nation in the world. The mission of these embassies and consulates is multifaceted and includes national security, assisting and protecting Americans living and traveling abroad, and advancing American policy interests.

There's no law that says a diplomat must have a college degree, but most of them have earned not only undergraduate college degrees but advanced degrees as well. English, economics, political science, and international studies all provide a good educational foundation for diplomatic work. Mastery of another language is also helpful, if not downright essential. Look beyond the basic Spanish and French into languages less commonly studied in U.S. schools such as Chinese, Russian, and Arabic.

Armed with the proper credentials and training, prospective diplomats are required to pass the foreign service exam—a tough test on such things as foreign affairs, English, writing, and management skills. Applicants who pass the exam move on through intensive background checks and an oral assessment of their temperament, people skills, and ability to interpret and report on events. Applicants who make it through this round are placed on a list of eligible candidates and are contacted when a position becomes available. Please note that of the more than 10,000 applicants who take the test every year, only about 300 are ever posted as diplomats. However, there are other kinds of positions available within the realm of the State Department, so keep your options open.

Those lucky few who make the final cut are hired as junior officers and spend several weeks at the National Foreign Affairs Training Center before being sent on their first overseas assignment. They sometimes receive foreign language instruction as well as an education in the history, customs, and culture of their assigned country. Overseas assignments last from about 18 months to four years. After that, a diplomat may be brought stateside for a tour or sent to another country.

Diplomats specialize in one of five specific areas or "cones." Cones are assigned or selected early in a diplomat's career and are more or less followed throughout a diplomat's career path.

Officers in administrative affairs are responsible for the daily operations of embassies and consulates. Their duties include overseeing budgeting, personnel, communications, and security.

Consular affairs officers help U.S. citizens who are traveling or living in their host country. They issue passports, register births and marriages of U.S. citizens, and keep locator information of Americans so they can be found and evacuated in case of an emergency. They also provide assistance for foreigners wanting to enter the United States.

Economic affairs diplomats collect, analyze, and report information relative to foreign economies. They must have an excellent understanding of the U.S. economy and the economy of their host nation.

Political affairs officers keep up with political events and conditions in their host country and report the same to the State Department. They also deliver official messages from the United States government to government officials in their host country.

Public diplomacy officers communicate between the United States and their host country. They promote U.S. interests and policies as well as attempt to give their host government an understanding of what America is all about.

These five areas are fairly diverse, but the State Department has identified skills and knowledge that are basic requirements for all diplomats. They include the following: proper English usage; knowledge of U.S. society, culture, history, government, political systems, the Constitution; and knowledge of world geography, international affairs, world political and social issues, basic accounting, statistics and mathematics, management, communication, and economics.

Junior officers or diplomats have a probationary period of four years. During this time, they are expected to satisfy foreign language requirements. If they pass muster, they are tenured, which means they can't be fired without a good reason. After receiving tenure, they can compete with other diplomats for choice assignments and promotions.

Anywhere, anytime is the creed of our nation's diplomats. Diplomats go where they are needed—even if it isn't exactly a dream location. Serving in developing nations with rough and sometimes dangerous living conditions is just as likely a scenario—if not more so—as black-tie state dinners with the queen of England.

Diplomats perform a valuable service to their country. It can be an exciting and challenging career choice—even noble at times. Globe-trotters who want to see the world and make a difference in world affairs may find the diplomatic corps a career to consider.

TRY IT OUT

REPORTING FOR DUTY!

Get on-line and go to a list of U.S. Embassies at http://usembassy.state.gov. Link to an embassy and learn everything you can about the economic and political conditions in a particular country. You can get more information about that country by using the CIA's *World Factbook* at www.odci.gov/cia/publications/factbook/index.html. Gather as much information as possible and then write a detailed report about the economy and politics of your country. Where are the hot spots? What are the big issues the country is grappling with? What is the United States doing to help?

DIPLOMACY IN ACTION

Diplomacy is a famous board game by Avalon Hills. You can probably find it at your local game and hobby shop. It is a strategy game that will allow you to test your aptitude for diplomacy as you try to take over the world. There are many groups who play on-line. You can get familiar with the on-line version at http://devel.diplom.org/DipPouch/Welcome.html.

SEE FOR YOURSELF

Watch a video about the challenges and rewards of a diplomatic career on-line at http://www.state.gov/www/careers/rfscareer.html#videos. Then check out some of the foreign service resources linked from that website.

- ☿ Get detailed information about a career as a foreign service officer from the State Department at http://www.state.gov/www/careers/rfscontents.html.
- ☿ Get details about the subjects covered on the Foreign Service Officer's Written Exam at http://www.state.gov/www/careers/rexample.html.
- ☿ Find links to diplomatic websites around the world at EmbassyWeb.com's site http://www.embpage.org.
- ☿ Get information about being a foreign service specialist at http://www.state.gov/www/careers/rfsspecover.html.

There are other websites full of useful information:

- ☿ Find out what's going on in the world of foreign policy at http://www.fpa.org.
- ☿ Read the *Foreign Service Journal* online at http://www.afsa.org/fsj.
- ☿ Find some diplomacy-related links at http://www.afsa.org/related.html.
- ☿ Check out the student section of the American Foreign Service Association's website at http://www.afsa.org/student.html.
- ☿ Learn about American foreign policy at http://www.unc.edu/depts/diplomat/.

GLOBAL READS

Here's a list of books about diplomacy to look for at your local library or bookstore. You may also want to look for resources about a specific place in the world.

Carland, Maria Pinto, and Michael Trucano. *Careers in International Affairs.* Washington, D.C.: Georgetown University Press, 1996.

Feltham, R. G. *Diplomatic Handbook.* Reading, Mass.: Addison-Wesley Publishing, 1994.

Fraser, Christine Hantel. *No Fixed Address: Life in the Foreign Service.* Toronto: University of Toronto Press, 1993.

Freeman, Charles W., Jr. *The Diplomat's Dictionary.* Washington, D.C.: Institute of Peace, 1997.

James, Sally. *Diplomatic Moves: Life in the Foreign Service.* New York: Palgrave, 1995.

Melbourne, Roy M. *Conflict and Crises: A Foreign Service Story.* Lanham, Md.: University Press of America, 1997.

Reeve, James, *Cocktails, Crises and Cockroaches: A Diplomatic Trail.* London: I B Tauris & Co. Ltd. 1999.

Scott, Gail, *Diplomatic Dance: The New Embassy Life in America.* Golden, Colo.: Fulcrum Publishing, 1999.

Simpson, Howard R. *Bush Hat, Black Tie: Adventures of a Foreign Service Officer:* New York: Brasseys, Inc., 1998.

Stearns, Monteagle. *Talking to Strangers.* Princeton, N.J.: Princeton University Press, 1999.

Steinberg, Eve P., and Arva C. Floyd. *American Foreign Service Officer (Arco Civil Service Test Tutor).* New York: Arco Publishing, 1992.

CHECK IT OUT

American Foreign Service Association
2101 E Street NW
Washington, D.C. 20037
http://www.afsa.org

Associates of the American Foreign Service Worldwide
5125 MacArthur Boulevard, Suite 36
Washington, D.C. 20016
http://www.aafsw.org

Executive Council on Foreign Diplomacy
818 Connecticut Avenue NW, 12th Floor
Washington, D.C. 20006

GET ACQUAINTED

Chuck Hunter, Diplomat

CAREER PATH

CHILDHOOD ASPIRATION: To be an author.

FIRST JOB: Cleaning up a clothing store and painting houses.

CURRENT JOB: Director of press relations for the U.S. State Department Bureau of Public Affairs.

A DEBATABLE CAREER CHOICE

Chuck Hunter is a self-professed "bookworm" and has been since he was a child. Back then he loved to read history and biographies, and he was especially fascinated to learn about the presidents.

Hunter also discovered an affinity for foreign languages when he got the opportunity to start studying French in sixth grade. He enjoyed the sound of putting new words together. In fact, he enjoyed it so much that he continued to study the language throughout high school and even pursued a double major in French and government in college.

Both these factors played a role in Hunter's career choice, but there was one additional detail that tipped the scales in favor of diplomacy: He got involved in his high school's speech and debate team. He discovered he was pretty good at it, and his coach encouraged Hunter to think about putting all these interests together as a foreign service officer.

SEEING (AND SERVING) THE WORLD

As soon as Hunter graduated from college, he jumped through all the hoops required to apply for a job with the State Department, and he passed every hurdle. However, while he was waiting for his background check to clear, he was offered a fellowship to attend graduate school at Stanford. It was an offer too good to refuse. Five years later, with a doctoral degree in French and the humanities firmly in hand, Hunter once again applied for a job as a diplomat. Once accepted, he chose an assignment in the public affairs cone.

Now, after more than 10 years of diplomatic service, Hunter has spent time in Algeria, Egypt, Tunisia, Oman, and Washington, D.C. His diplomatic career started with a year of language training in Washington, D.C., followed by tours in Egypt and Algeria, where he served as assistant public affairs officer. The Algerian tour was abbreviated when civil unrest broke out and 50 percent of the Americans working at the embassy were evacuated. After a brief stint in D.C., Hunter was back for another year of language study in Tunisia and a three-year posting as public affairs officer in Oman. Stateside duties have included serving in the Near Eastern Affairs office, with responsibilities to keep tabs on things in Amman, Beirut, Jerusalem, Tel Aviv, and Damascus, and his current position as director of press relations for the State Department's Bureau of Public Affairs.

So far, Algeria is the only post where his proficiency in French has been called upon. But that's the result of a carefully calculated decision Hunter made early on. Looking at the options, Hunter realized that the Middle East is an important place in diplomatic terms. He felt certain that work in that region was likely to "really matter" in world affairs. So he took the plunge and volunteered to specialize in Arabic (one of four languages that the State Department considers "super" hard—the others being Chinese, Japanese, and Korean). It's a decision Hunter has yet to regret as he continues to view events in the Middle East as pivotal to the rest of the world.

DIPLOMATIC NEGOTIATIONS

Hunter has a few suggestions for young people hoping for a diplomatic future. Although learning another language is an obvious suggestion, Hunter says it's more than just learning words; he's found that learning to understand the language of another culture is a huge step toward understanding the people and making sense of a system that is different from your own. He also thinks it's important to learn about life outside the United States. As citizens of the world's superpower, Americans have so much—a good standard of living and good government—that it's easy to get wrapped up in our own little world, according to Hunter. Awareness of other peoples and places can help cultivate the openness and tolerance necessary to contribute to and live in a world of peace, stability, and security.

Oh, and one more thing while you're at it. How about asking your parents to get you a passport for your next birthday? It's not that expensive, it's valid for 10 years, and who knows when you might need it!

Event Planner

WHAT IS AN EVENT PLANNER?

Meetings make the business world go around. Event planners make sure all those meetings go well—whether it's a convention, seminar, sales meeting, product introduction, or celebration.

Event and meeting planners work in different ways to get the job done. Some are on the staff of a large corporation. Their primary responsibility is to plan meetings and special events for various departments in the company. Anything from arranging an incentive trip to Hawaii to planning a training seminar to hosting the company holiday party might fall under a corporate meeting planner's job description.

Other meeting planners work for professional associations and may be responsible for planning a huge annual convention involving thousands of members, hundreds of special workshop sessions and exhibitors, and all kinds of special events. Marketing the convention to association members and keeping track of registration information may come with the territory as well.

Another type of event planner works for (or owns) an event planning company. Some of these companies specialize in arranging incentive trips to wonderful locations for clients who want to reward their staff or colleagues, while others focus on planning fund-raising galas for charity organizations or other types of special events.

The one thing that all meeting planners have in common is details—and plenty of them. It starts with lots of questions: What type of event does the client have in mind? Where will it be held? How many people do they expect to attend? What is the project budget? And on and on the questions go.

As questions get answered, a theme often starts to emerge, and then the real planning begins. The meeting planner plans down to the last detail. After developing a budget, the first big decision is deciding where the event will take place. This is where the travel comes in. Event planners frequently make trips to check out potential event locations. They might look at several different hotels or convention centers to see which can best meet the needs of the event.

Food is an important part of most meetings and events, so menu selection is another big decision. Depending on the kind of event, planners may line up speakers, special training sessions, recreational activities, and entertainment. They also

arrange for any necessary audiovisual, lighting, or sound equipment. Then there are the decorators, florists, and security considerations to be determined. Don't forget that out-of-town guests may need transportation and hotel arrangements!

No matter what type of event, meeting and event planners can expect to arrive early and leave late. Early arrival assures that everything is ready to roll when the event begins. The mark of a well-planned event is one that runs smoothly. Good meeting planners make their jobs look easy by making sure that even the smallest details are handled without a glitch. After the event is over, there is still work to do. Supervising clean-up and paying suppliers are part of the follow-up process, as is some sort of evaluation or final report to the client.

Event planners tend to be very creative and well organized. They have excellent contacts and communications skills. Since meeting planners also work with budgets, a head for figures is also required.

It used to be that most meeting and event planners learned the tricks of the trade on the job while working as an assistant to an experienced planner. Some still do. Increasingly, however, meeting and event planners are finding that a degree in hospitality or event or meeting management gives them the edge they need in this competitive industry. Earning certificates in programs offered by Meeting Planners International or the International Special Events Society provides some extra clout on the résumé too. Both of these credentials require experience in the field and successful completion of a written exam.

TRY IT OUT

JOIN THE CLUB

Get your start by planning meetings and events at your school or place of worship. There are probably dozens of clubs that have weekly or monthly meetings and special events. Join one and volunteer to help plan an upcoming meeting. Be sure to get involved with the committee that plans the school dances too!

PARTY!

Get your parents' permission to host a party at home. Make a checklist of all the details you have to arrange, such as invitations, food, drinks, decorations, and entertainment. Try to come up with a unique theme for your event and find creative ways to carry it out. After your party, get feedback from your guests about what they liked and disliked. Make notes throughout the process so your next party will be easier to plan.

PARTY 2!

Imagine you are a professional meeting planner and you have been hired by a software company to plan a huge party to introduce the media to their latest and greatest product. They want to make a huge splash and money is no object. You'll need to select a site that will accommodate 2,000 guests, fabulous food and beverages, and top-notch entertainment. You'll need a blockbuster theme and the decorations to pull it off. Just for fun, when you've got it all planned out, design a knock-out invitation so that no one in their right mind will want to miss your party. Get in gear and use these on-line resources to plan this spectacular event.

Use the room-size calculator at http://www.mpiweb.org/net/calc.htm to find out what size room you'll need for your event and let your imagination take over from there.

VIRTUAL MEETING PLANNER

There are a lot of other interesting sites for meeting planners that are worth a look. Start with these:

- ☼ Search for job listings by region at http://www.pcma.org/toolbox/jobs/default.htm.
- ☼ Find sample checklists, modeling contracts, and a glossary of meeting terms at http://www.pcma.org/toolbox/splash.htm.
- ☼ ConventionPlanner.com at http://www.conventionplanner.com will connect you to people, resources, and suppliers needed to plan a convention,

event, or meeting in most big cities around the country.

☀ Read about some successful meetings and events (and look at the pictures) at http://www. yournextmeeting.com/success-stories.htm.

☀ Find more resources for planners at Industry Meeting Network at http://www.industry meetings.com/ resources.html.

☀ Get some tips at http://www.meetingplannertips.com.

☀ Flip through the pages of *Meetings and Conventions* magazine on-line at http://www.meetings-conventions.com/main.html.

☀ Get the scoop on on-line learning courses for meeting planners at http://www.mpiweb.org/distance.htm.

☀ Learn the qualifications for the Event Management Certification program at the George Washington University at http://www.gwu.edu/~cpd/programs/ CWEP/index.html.

☀ See how meeting professionals are helping people in need at Network for the Needy at http://www.pcma. org/nftn/default.htm.

BOOKS ON BOOKING

Read all about meeting and event planning. Here are some books to get you started.

Allen, Judy. *Event Planning: The Ultimate Guide to Successful Meetings, Corporate Events, Fundraising Galas, Conferences, Incentives and Other Special Events.* New York: John Wiley & Sons, 2000.

Boehme, Ann J. Plannin. *Successful Meetings and Events: A Take-Charge Assistant Book.* New York: AMACOM, 1998.

Goldblatt, Joe Jeff. *Special Events: Best Practices in Modern Event Management.* New York: John Wiley & Sons, 1997.

Goldblatt, Joe Jeff, and Frank Supovitz. *Dollars & Events: How to Succeed in the Special Events Business.* New York: John Wiley & Sons, 1999.

McMahon, Tom. *Big Meetings Big Results: Strategic Event Planning for Productivity and Profit.* Lincolnwood, Ill.: NTC Publishing Group, 1996.

Van Kirk, Richard L. *The Complete Guide to Special Event Management: Business Insights, Financial Advice and Successful Strategies from Ernst & Young.* New York: John Wiley & Sons, 1992.

Warner, Diane. *Diane Warner's Big Book of Parties: Creative Party Planning for Every Occasion.* Hawthorne, N.J.: Career Press, 1999.

CHECK IT OUT

Alliance of Meeting Management Consultants
P.O. Box 986
Irmo, South Carolina 29063
http://www.ammc.org

International Special Events Society
9202 N. Meridan Street, Suite 200
Indianapolis, Indiana 46260
http://www.ises.com

International Society of Meeting Planners
8383 E. Evans Road
Scottsdale, Arizona 85260
http://www.iami.org

Meeting Professionals International
4455 LBJ Freeway, Suite 1200
Dallas, Texas 75244
http://www.mpiweb.org

The Professional Convention Management Association
100 Vestavia Parkway, Suite 220
Birmingham, Alabama 35216-3743
http://www.pcma.org

Society of Corporate Meeting Planners
1819 Peachtree Street NE, Suite 620
Atlanta, Georgia 30309

GET ACQUAINTED

Shelley Matheny, Event Planner

CAREER PATH

CHILDHOOD ASPIRATION: To work with children and travel.

FIRST JOB: Folding towels in her aunt's beauty salon.

CURRENT JOB: President and CEO of KidsAlong, Inc.

THE ACCIDENTAL MEETING PLANNER

Shelley Matheny didn't plan on becoming an event planner; she sort of got thrown into it after graduating from college with a business degree. She answered an ad for an administrative assistant job that, unknown to her at the time, had been placed by one of the world's largest incentive travel agencies. She got the job, loved it, and within two weeks was actually planning events. A couple years later, she moved on to a smaller company where she was responsible for planning events from start to finish, which proved to be a great way to learn more about the event planning process.

When that company went out of business, she was hired to join the special events and conferences staff of a large corporation. At that time, the company's in-house event planning division was known as the best in the business. It was such a large operation that it included an entire department to cover airline arrangements, another department to handle conference registrations, and eight meeting planners. This job turned out to be Matheny's dream come true. She traveled all over the world managing eight to 10 different conferences.

HAVE CHILDREN, WILL TRAVEL

From the very first job, Matheny knew she wanted to be a meeting planner. But after giving birth to her second child,

Matheny needed a job with more flexibility. Starting her own meeting planning business—where she could pick and choose when and where her time was spent—was the next logical step in her career path.

She found just the right twist for her business when a large company asked her to put together a program for the 150 children who would be accompanying their parents to a conference in Hawaii. Matheny put together a winning children's program complete with adventure hikes, tennis workshops, hula lessons, painting coconuts, treasure hunts, and making leis. When Matheny realized that she'd had just as much fun as the kids, she knew she was on to something for her own business.

That's when KidsAlong, Inc. was born. The company specializes in providing imaginative children's programs for meetings and conferences. Matheny says that her job requires all the meeting skills that she's acquired along the way—and then some. Matheny's business handles about 25 events each year involving anywhere from 30 to 1,500 children in places all over the world. American cities such as Palm Springs, San Francisco, New York City, Hilton Head, and New Orleans have been home to some of Matheny's programs, while Canada, Mexico, Austria, and Italy are some of the far-flung locations her work has taken her. No matter where the meeting is held, no two events are ever the same. Each program is custom designed and extra special.

THE RIGHT STUFF

Matheny doesn't mean to brag or anything, but she thinks she's got a great job. She says that it probably never occurs to a lot of kids that there is a real career out there called "meeting planner." But there is, and Matheny heartily recommends it.

She says that many schools even offer training programs just for meeting planners. As for Matheny, she learned how to do it by actually doing it. But she did take the time to complete the requirements to obtain a "Certified Meeting Planner" credential. It's a designation that indicates to clients that she knows what she's doing and shows a certain commitment to her profession.

If you'd like to know more Matheny's really cool job, you can visit her website at http://www.kidsalong.com.

Foreign Correspondent

WHAT IS A FOREIGN CORRESPONDENT?

Foreign correspondents are journalists who report news and events from other countries. Their jobs involve travel, excitement, danger, intrigue, and historic events.

Foreign correspondents report for newspapers, magazines, cable and television networks, radio broadcasts, news wires, and on-line news services. They are first and foremost reporters, and their work is similar in many ways to the work of counterparts who work in the United States. The biggest difference is that foreign correspondents do their reporting from other parts of the world.

Like other journalists, foreign correspondents go after newsworthy stories and sometimes have to go to great lengths to get them. They collect information through research, interviews, and contacts. They analyze this information and write stories that are clear, factual, and free from personal bias. Their stories cover all the bases of who, what, where, when, why, and how.

With foreign correspondents often covering volatile parts of the world, there's no room for mistakes. Facts must be checked and rechecked. Not only are the journalists' reputations on the line, but, quite often, important aspects of our nation's international relations hinge on accurate reporting of current events; foreign correspondents are our nation's eyes and ears in other parts of the world.

Getting the inside scoop depends on being in the right place, at the right time, with the right contacts. Some reporters are assigned to cover the foreign "desk" of a particular country or region of the world, which allows for "on the spot" coverage as significant events take place. Other correspondents move from place to place, following big, breaking news stories.

It is not uncommon for foreign correspondents to find themselves in war zones. They often get to see history unfold before their eyes. Many have literally put their lives in danger to get the story. More than one foreign correspondent has lost his or her life in the line of duty.

Exceptional written and oral communication skills are critical for foreign correspondents. A knowledge of history and international affairs and an understanding of other cultures and political systems are also essential. It doesn't hurt to be fluent in another language or two as well.

It's probably no surprise to learn that foreign correspondence is not the typical nine-to-five kind of job. Foreign

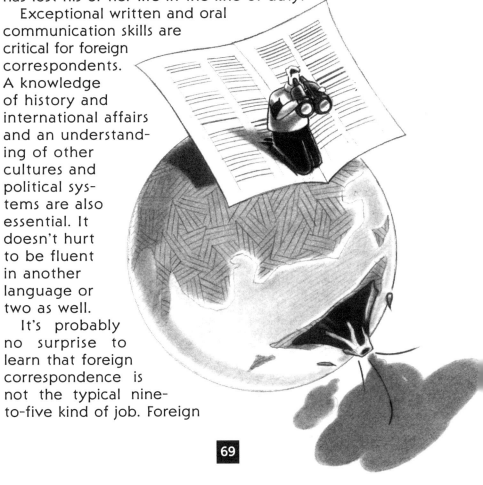

correspondents work when and where news is breaking, even if that means round-the-clock coverage of a big story. They tend to keep their bags packed in case they have to get to a story on a moment's notice. Deadlines can create tremendous pressure. However, quiet news days offer opportunities for sniffing out leads, cultivating contacts, and enjoying other places in the world.

Foreign correspondents need a college degree in a subject such as journalism, English, communications, political science, or history. It is very uncommon for someone to be hired as a foreign correspondent right out of school. Most earn their stripes working at smaller papers, move to larger, national news organizations, and eventually land jobs as foreign correspondents after lots of hard work.

Foreign correspondents keep the world informed about what's happening in other places. Their work helps shape our perception of the world, and it is often instrumental in shaping foreign policy and affecting change. Whether it's some sort of social injustice, a natural disaster, or all-out war, foreign correspondents are on the spot to get the word out.

TRY IT OUT!

THE WRITE STUFF

Start getting the valuable writing experience you'll need as a foreign correspondent by writing for your school newspaper. Also, contact the editor of your hometown paper and see if they accept articles from students. You may be able to submit stories about sports and other school activities for publication. Don't forget to clip (cut out and save) your published articles so you can start your portfolio.

SNIFF OUT A STORY

Sniff out an international event on the Web. Research and gather facts from several sources and write a story.

Reuters at http://www.reuters.com is a good source for the latest international news.

You'll also find up-to-the minute reports at

- http://www.cnn.com
- http://www.abc.com/news
- http://www.cbs.news.com
- http://www.nbc.com/news
- http://www.usatoday.com

Compare U.S. coverage of a story with coverage from newspapers around the world at http://worldnewspapers. about.com/newsissues/worldnewspapers/index.htm/rnk= c4&terms=journalism.

READ ALL ABOUT IT

Read a fascinating article about journalist Martha Gellhorn at http://www.freedomforum.org/international/1998/2/ gellhorn_interview.asp. She was a foreign correspondent for more than 60 years and covered the Spanish Civil War, World War II, and Vietnam.

GET THE SCOOP

Other Web resources for foreign correspondents-in-the-making are:

- Use the Foreign Correspondents' site at http://www.uq.edu.au/jrn/fc/ for a collection of links to country and government information.
- Get more guidance on "How to Become a Foreign Correspondent—Without Leaving Home!" at http://www.inkspot.com/feature/foreign.html.
- Read the on-line book *50 Miles to the Page: How to Be a Freelance Foreign Correspondent* at http:// www.booklocker.com/bookpages/adambrown01.html.
- Check out a newsroom just for students with some cool activities at http://www.writesite.org/html/ newsroom.html.
- Travel with foreign correspondents at http://www.abc. net.au/foreign for a colorful look at the culture and

lifestyle of people who don't make international head-lines. Don't forget to check out their links page.

AN ARMCHAIR ADVENTURE

Here's a list of just a few of the many books about journalism in general and foreign correspondence in particular. See what you can find at your local library or bookstore.

Beeston, Richard. *Looking for Trouble: The Life and Times of a Foreign Correspondent.* Dulles, Va.: Brassey's Inc., 1997.

Cappon, Rene J. *Associated Press Guide to News Writing.* New York: ARCO Publishing, 2000.

Fox, Walter. *Writing the News: A Guide for Print Journalists.* Ames, Iowa: Iowa State University Press, 1998.

Goodman, Alan, and John Pollack. *The World on a String: How to Become a Freelance Foreign Correspondent.* New York: Henry Holt, 1997.

Gruber, Ruth. *Ahead of Time: My Early Years as a Foreign Correspondent.* New York: Carroll & Graf, 2001.

Harsch, Joseph C., and Joseph Fromm. *At the Hinge of History: A Reporter's Story.* Athens, Ga.: University of Georgia Press, 1993.

Hess, Stephen. *International News and Foreign Correspondents, Volume 5.* Washington, D.C.: Brookings Institution Press, 1996.

Metzler, Ken. *Creative Interviewing: The Writer's Guide to Gathering Information by Asking Questions.* Needham Heights, Mass.: Allyn & Bacon, 1996.

Redmont, Bernard S. *Risks Worth Taking: The Odyssey of a Foreign Correspondent.* Lanham, Md.: University Press of America, 1992.

Yorke, Ivor. *Basic TV Reporting.* Woburn, Mass.: Focal Press, 1997.

CHECK IT OUT

International Federation of Journalists
266 rue Royale
1210 Brussels, Belgium
http://www.ifj.org

National Association of Broadcasters
1771 N Street NW
Washington, D.C. 20036
http://www.nab.org

The Newspaper Guild
501 Third Street
Washington, D.C. 20001
http://www.newsguild.org

The Overseas Press Club of America
40 West 45th Street
New York, New York 10036
http://www.opcofamerica.org

Society of Professional Journalists
16 South Jackson Street
Greencastle, Indiana 46135
http://www.spj.org

GET ACQUAINTED

Alison Smale,
Foreign Correspondent

CAREER PATH

CHILDHOOD ASPIRATION: To be an archaeologist.

FIRST JOB: Usher at a local movie theater.

CURRENT JOB: Assistant foreign editor with the *New York Times*.

A FAMILY TRADITION

Alison Smale grew up in England where her father was a financial reporter. She thought his job seemed nice enough since it allowed him to go places and meet interesting people. As a child, she had always thought she wanted to be an archaeologist. But when she turned 16 and everyone else seemed to have a plan for their lives, it was a logical leap to announce journalism as her goal. And why not? It didn't require as much patience as being an archaeologist did!

Smale's college majors were German and political science and included one year of study in Germany. After graduating, Smale decided she wanted to see America—not the America tourists saw during three weeks aboard a Greyhound bus, but the real America. The opportunity to do just that presented itself in the form of a full scholarship to study for a master's degree at Stanford University.

Her studies in the United States proved to be a wonderful experience and eventually led to her first job as a foreign correspondent. Part of her training involved an internship with United Press International (UPI), an international news wire service, in Germany and London. After she graduated she was offered the chance to return to Germany to run the Bonn office—quite an accomplishment for such a young reporter.

THE WORLD ACCORDING TO SMALE
While in Germany, she covered such historic events as Iran's release of U.S. hostages, the royal wedding of Prince Charles and the late Princess Diana, and issues related to the cold war as they played out in East Germany. She also accepted a job with the Associated Press (AP), another worldwide news service.

This new allegiance led to a coveted job in Moscow. Long fascinated by the Soviet Union and affairs in Eastern Europe, Smale found herself right in the middle of some of the most pivotal times in that region's recent history. She had a first-hand look at what it was like to live in communist countries, and she was there to see the struggles of many of those countries to regain their freedom.

A RUSSIAN ROMANCE
It was while she was in Russia that she met and fell in love with a Russian pianist and composer—much to the chagrin of

the KGB. Russian's infamous secret police didn't favor the relationship. After all, Smale was a foreign correspondent, suspicious in and of itself. The couple responded by being as open as possible about their relationship, despite pressures from the KGB.

Things really came to a head when the couple married and Smale was assigned to a new job in Vienna. At first, the Russian government refused to grant Smale's husband a visa so that he could go with her. Knowing that she had a choice to make, Smale opted to work within the system instead of making a major fuss about it in international headlines. Her subtle approach won out in the end, her husband received a visa, and Smale says she learned a valuable lesson in the process. She says she discovered that, if you really believe in something or love someone, you can always find a way to make things work out.

NEXT STOP—VIENNA

Smale's next assignment was in Vienna. She was AP's bureau chief for Eastern Europe and led a staff of some 70 reporters. It was a heady time to be in this part of the world as communism fell in country after country. War erupted in Yugoslavia during Smale's Eastern Europe assignment. She said it was horrifying to see a wonderful country deteriorate into mindless destruction as neighbor fought neighbor while the rest of the world tried to pretend nothing was wrong. Smale found the only way to fight the fear was to work, work, work, and to try not to think about the awful things she was covering in her stories.

While she's seen her share of danger and excitement as a journalist, Smale says she learned always to have a way out before she put herself in harm's way. She'd take necessary precautions such as wearing a flak jacket and helmet, but she says there's really only way to keep yourself out of danger and that is to THINK. Yes, she's had a few close calls and even experienced a sniper attack in Sarajevo (no one in the press car was injured), but she always seemed to manage to get out in time.

A CHANGE OF PACE

Smale's current role in world affairs is as assistant foreign editor for the *New York Times*. She is responsible for putting out the weekend editions of the foreign affairs section of this major newspaper. While a desk in a New York City newsroom is a bit removed from the front line of a war zone, Smale says it represents a natural progression in her career and gives her more time for her husband and young daughter (born just a month after the Bosnian war broke out).

If you'd like to read some of Smale's work, go on-line and run a search for "Alison Smale" to access some of her front-line reports, or pick up a Sunday edition of the *New York Times* for a more current version of Smale's take on world issues.

International Businessperson

SHORTCUTS

SKILL SET

✔ MONEY

✔ TRAVEL

✔ ADVENTURE

GO to a big department store and read the labels on various products to see where they were made.

READ the business section of a major newspaper to find out what's happening in the world of business.

TRY getting to know a foreign exchange student at your school to learn about a different culture.

WHAT IS AN INTERNATIONAL BUSINESSPERSON?

It's a small world, and thanks to innovations in transportation, communications, and technology the world is becoming one big marketplace. Never before have there been so many ways to see the world at work.

Virtually any job you can do in your homeland, you can do abroad. Increasing numbers of American companies have branch offices in overseas locations (and vice versa), which means that someone has to do the same jobs there that get done here and everything from janitor to CEO is up for grabs. International jobs require actually relocating to a new place to live and work in another culture.

Another kind of international business opportunity involves being based in one country and making occasional or frequent trips to other countries. Thousands of businesspeople function in this way—whether it's a publisher working with an overseas printer or a banker investing in overseas businesses. This type of situation often offers the best of both worlds— the excitement of global travel with all the comforts of home just a flight away.

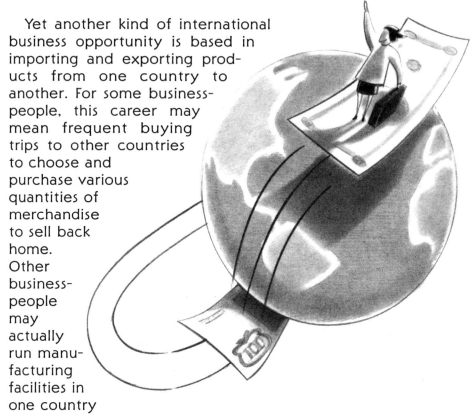

Yet another kind of international business opportunity is based in importing and exporting products from one country to another. For some business-people, this career may mean frequent buying trips to other countries to choose and purchase various quantities of merchandise to sell back home. Other business-people may actually run manu-facturing facilities in one country to produce products that will be sold in another.

While the educational route necessary to prepare for a career in international business is as varied as the available occupations, most successful globe-trotters share a few common traits, such as good analytical and organizational skills, strong oral and written communication skills, computer literacy, fluency in languages, and strong interpersonal skills. It also helps to be self-starting, adaptable, and flexible.

Beyond that there are many avenues for training. Foreign language fluency (in at least one language) and an MBA will equip you for some of the most lucrative international jobs. You could try undergraduate work in economics, business, marketing, or in a specialized field such as textiles or manu-facturing. Or if you are absolutely certain of your goals, get a degree in international business. A good program will cover subjects such as accounting, marketing, finance, and management.

By its very nature, international business tends to require quite a bit of globe-trotting. Getting from your home state, wherever it may be, to Europe, Asia, or Latin America is no small feat. Take this little quiz to see if you've got what it takes to be a world traveler:

- Bad hair days become the norm when traveling in countries that don't accommodate your electrical "personal grooming appliances." Can you deal with it? Yes or No
- Sushi, kimchi? No matter how unusual or exotic the native food gets, just bring it on! Yes or No
- There's nothing like a good night's sleep aboard a roaring 747. Sound like a dream to you? Yes or No
- Finding your way in a place where few others speak your language would challenge you in a positive way? Yes or No
- Adjusting your habits and manners to those considered acceptable in your host country—is that something you can deal with comfortably? Yes or No

Those questions touch on some of the issues that international businesspeople encounter every day. Although they may seem insignificant, combined with the ordinary pressures of any job, they can have a major impact on a person's job satisfaction and performance.

However, adding some international flair to any kind of career choice can be an enriching experience—in more ways than one. Think about it. Are you ready to work your way around the world?

TRY IT OUT

BUSINESS BRIEFING

Pick a country, any country. Then go on-line and to the library to find out as much information as you can about the types of products they make and those they bring in from other places. A great source of information is the Global Business Factbook found at http://www.globalbusiness.about.com/money/globalbusiness/library/ gbf/bl_gbf.htm.

Pretend you need to brief the CEO of your company for a business trip, and compile everything you find in a notebook.

CLICK AROUND THE WORLD

For access to all kinds of information about international business, go to www.about.com and run a search for "international business."

For the latest news in the business world, visit websites such as these:

☀ CNN Online News at http://www.cnn.com
☀ *Wall Street Journal* at http://www.wsj.com
☀ *USA Today* at http://www.usatoday.com

MIND YOUR MANNERS

When doing business in other parts of the world, it always pays to know what the local version of "Miss Manners" has to say about polite behavior. Polite in one place might be considered outrageous someplace else. It is never fun (or profitable) to be on the wrong side of a cultural faux pas.

Books that will help you keep your cultural ducks in a row include:

Axtell, Roger. *Do's and Taboos Around the World.* New York: John Wiley & Sons, 1993.

Morrison, Terri, Wayne Conaway, and Joseph Douress. *Dun & Bradstreet's Guide to Doing Business Around the World.* Upper Saddle River, N.J.: Prentice Hall Press, 2000.

Morrison, Terri, Wayne Conaway, and George Borden. *Kiss, Bow, or Shake Hands: How to Do Business in Sixty Countries.* Holbrook, Mass.: Adams Media Corp., 1995.

If you prefer on-line resources, you can find all kinds of tips for doing business abroad at http://www.getcustoms.com/onmibus/dba.html. Compare the differences among places such as Argentina, Hong Kong, and Sweden.

Another great on-line source of information is the International Study and Travel Center at http://www.istc.umn.edu/default.html. Don't leave home with it!

TRADING PLACES

Participating in an international student exchange program is a great way to explore new cultures. You can either visit a foreign country or host a foreign student at your house. Either way, you'll learn more about other people and places in the world. For information about these kinds of opportunities, visit these websites or conduct a search for "foreign exchange student."

- American Institute for Foreign Study at http://www.aifs.org.
- ASSE International Student Exchange Program at http://www.asse.com
- American International Youth Student Exchange Program at http://www.aiysep.org
- Youth for Understanding International Exchange at http://www.yfu.org

Use with parental guidance only.

CHECK IT OUT

Academy of International Business
College of Business Administration
University of Hawaii at Manoa
2404 Maile Way
Honolulu, Hawaii 96822
http://www.aibworld.net

Association for International Business
725 G Street
Salida, Colorado 81201
http://www.aib-world.org

U.S. Council for International Business
1212 Avenue of the Americas
New York, New York 10036
http://www.uscib.org

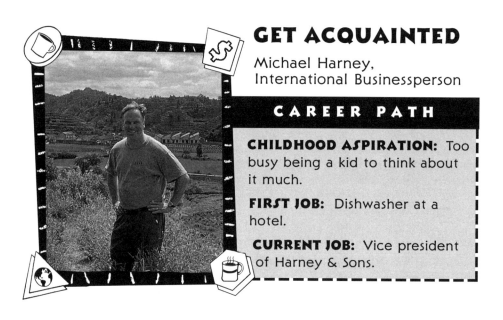

GET ACQUAINTED

Michael Harney,
International Businessperson

CAREER PATH

CHILDHOOD ASPIRATION: Too busy being a kid to think about it much.

FIRST JOB: Dishwasher at a hotel.

CURRENT JOB: Vice president of Harney & Sons.

Michael Harney graduated from Cornell University with a degree in hotel management. He was lucky enough to land his first big job in Paris, where he worked in a wine-related tourism business. The job entailed a little of this and a little of that, and it eventually resulted in his working as a wine taster. Next on Harney's career map was a stop in the accounting department at a resort in the Virgin Islands. That was followed by eight years in Chicago where he ran a small boutique hotel that catered to an international clientele.

A FAMILY TRADITION

In the meantime, Harney's father had built a gourmet tea company back home in Connecticut and needed some help. With a business called Harney & Sons, Harney was the only man for the job (since his brother already worked there).

Now Harney is a vital part of the thriving business. As the company website explains, Harney "travels the world searching for renowned varieties as well as exciting new infusions, from Germany to India," and recent trips were made to China and France—all in a quest to find the perfect teas!

JUST A SPOT OF TEA

Tea taster is one of Harney's most important functions at the company. To do it right, he measures a dime's worth of tea into a cup of hot water and lets it brew for five minutes. Then he uses several senses to evaluate the results. First, he looks at the remains of the loose tea leaves. Then comes the most important step—smelling it. Taste is the last step. But, like wine tasters, tea tasters don't gulp down a sample; instead, they swish it around in their mouths and then spit it out.

How does Harney judge whether it's good tea or not? Experience helps, but the true test of a good tea is one that makes your mouth move up into a smile.

A BIG WORLD OUT THERE

All things considered, Harney thinks it's a great time to be an American doing business around the world. Even though many of the people he trades with can speak English, Harney makes a point of learning at least a few phrases in the host country's language. It's a way to show respect for them. He also tries to understand where they are coming from by learning as much as he can about their country and culture.

To see photos from one of Harney's latest trips abroad, go to the company website at http://www.harney.com/harneyteas/travel.html.

International Relief Worker

SHORTCUTS

GO to the video store and rent the movie *Volunteers* for a humorous look at relief work.

READ *100 Jobs in Social Change* by Harley Jebens (New York: IDG Books, 1997).

TRY volunteering for a local relief organization.

WHAT IS AN INTERNATIONAL RELIEF WORKER?

For people in trouble, international relief workers are often the human equivalent of Superman. Among the first ones on the scene of the world's most dire situations, these people are quite often—and quite literally—lifesavers. The help extended by international relief workers takes many different forms, for instance:

An international relief worker is a doctor who gives desperately needed medical care to children and families in underdeveloped and impoverished areas of the world.

An international relief worker is a Peace Corps volunteer helping farmers grow healthy food for their communities.

An international relief worker is a carpenter working with organizations such as Habitat for Humanity to build decent, affordable housing all around the world.

An international relief worker is part of a Red Cross team that travels anywhere in the world on a moment's notice when disaster strikes. They bring food and clean water, and they assist with cleanup.

An international relief worker is a teacher teaching English or any number of other subjects in schools found in both large cities and small villages around the world.

An international relief worker delivers shoe boxes lovingly packed with toys, candy, and toiletries to children in war-torn areas who wouldn't have them otherwise.

And, an international relief worker provides aid to victims of violent conflicts—sometimes at considerable risk to themselves.

These are just a handful of jobs that are performed by international relief workers; there are many more. Just as there are many different kinds of international relief jobs, there are many different international relief organizations ranging from religious organizations to groups that protect human rights or the environment. All this diversity provides an amazing array of opportunities for people with all kinds of talents, education, and experience. Blending personal passions with a profession is what this kind of work is all about.

There are also many different career paths for an international relief worker, depending on what you want to do. Useful college degrees include education, engineering, agriculture, medicine, and social sciences. Some positions require master's degrees. Other positions call for skill in trades such as plumbing, electrical wiring, or carpentry.

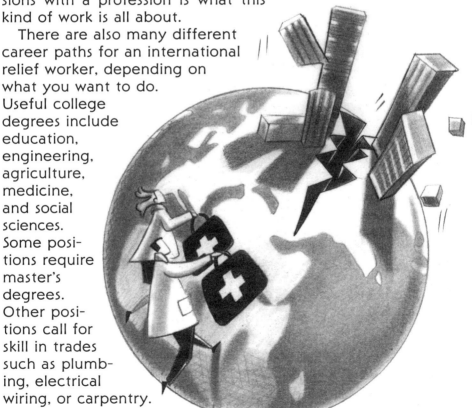

In addition, almost any type of administrative or managerial position available in other types of organizations is also available in international relief agencies. These include program directors who manage various projects or departments, development directors who raise money to support relief efforts, and volunteer coordinators who organize the volunteers.

Speaking of volunteers, many international relief workers volunteer their services on a part-time basis. They have "regular" jobs most of the year and go on relief trips during their vacation time. For example, a lot of doctors with thriving practices in the United States volunteer a few weeks every year to offer medical services to needy people in every corner of the world. For those with families or those who can't afford to do relief work full-time, these short-term trips are a great way to make the world a better place.

International relief work is not a route to monetary riches. For example, the Peace Corps pays living expenses for volunteers, and at the end of their assignments they receive $200 for each month they served. Most assignments last two years. Any way you add the numbers, it's no way to get rich quick. However, the experience itself can be invaluable when it comes time to look for other types of work.

International relief workers often see parts of the world that most people never see. And they go to sleep at night knowing they have made a significant contribution to their world—a feeling that money can't buy.

TRY IT OUT

HERE I COME TO SAVE THE DAY!

Visit AlertNet at http://www.alertnet.org. It has the latest news and up-to-date information on disaster and relief efforts around the world. Acquaint yourself with a crisis and identify a group needing aid. Imagine you are in charge of a relief organization that wants to help.

You will have to answer a lot of questions: What kinds of volunteers are needed? Medical? Technical? Construction crews? Do they need food, building materials, medical supplies, or clothing? What other resources will you need to provide relief? How will you recruit the volunteers that you need?

Prepare a disaster relief plan outlining the needs and how you will meet them.

GO AHEAD, CHANGE THE WORLD

Talk is cheap. If you really want to make a difference, start now. If you begin looking now, chances are good that you can find a relief project to work on during your next summer vacation. An international trip may be as close as your local school or place of worship. Many churches offer teenagers an opportunity to participate in summer mission trips. Check it out! If that doesn't work out, there are some resources you can check on-line.

International World Changers (http://www.thetask.org/iwc. htm) sponsor youth trips every summer to places such as Kenya, Jordan, South Africa, and Sudan. Students participate in activities such as construction, English language camps, boys and girls clubs, sports outreach, and scripture distribution.

Habitat for Humanity International (http://www.habitat. org/GV/) offers international trips through their Global Village Program. Participants around the world work with locals to build decent and affordable housing.

Or go ahead and start your own Kids Care Club. Find out how at http:///www.kidscare.org.

CHARITY BEGINS AT HOME

Maybe an international trip is not in your immediate future. There are plenty of opportunities for you to get a taste for relief work right here. There are probably some right in your hometown. Check your phone book for local chapters of the American Red Cross, Habitat for Humanity, and the Salvation Army. Rescue missions and soup kitchens are always in need of volunteers. Your local Junior League can also point you in the direction of some local volunteer jobs. Even if after volunteering you decide that a career in relief work is not for you, the experience you gain will be valuable to you regardless of your career choice.

Spend some time on-line for more info on international relief work. Here are some sites to get you started.

- ☼ Find links to members of InterAction, the nation's largest coalition of relief, development, and refugee agencies, at http://www.interaction.org/members/index.html.
- ☼ Watch a short video on-line about children in Romania at the Children's Relief Network site at http://www.romanianchildren.org.
- ☼ Link to different relief organizations from Reliefnet at http://www.reliefnet.org.
- ☼ Search through a database of jobs in disaster relief at http://www.alertnet.org/alertjobs.
- ☼ Jobs with Nonprofits: A Guide at http://www.pratt.lib.md.us/slrc/job/nonprofit.html is an online resource for job-hunting at nonprofit organizations.
- ☼ Take a virtual tour of a refugee camp and find out about the work that Doctors without Borders does at http://www.dwb.org.
- ☼ Join Amnesty International and their international human rights movement at http://www.amnestyusa.org.
- ☼ Samaritan's Purse is a nondenominational evangelical Christian organization that provides spiritual and physical aid to needy people around the world. See what they are up to at http://www.samaritanspurse.org.
- ☼ Learn everything you ever wanted to know about the Peace Corps at http://www.peacecorps.gov. Be sure to check out the special kids section.
- ☼ The American Red Cross site at http://www.redcross.org will give you some insight into the many different kinds of relief work that they do.
- ☼ CARE is one of the world's largest private international relief and development organizations. You will find them on the web at http://www.care.org.

GOOD READS ON DOING GOOD

Check out some of the diverse opportunities for long- and short-term international relief work with some of these titles.

Banerjee, Dillon. *So You Want to Join the Peace Corps: What to Know Before You Go.* Berkeley, Calif.: Ten Speed Press, 2000.

Benjamin, Medea, and Miya Rodolfo-Sioson. *The Peace Corps and More: 175 Ways to Work, Study and Travel at Home & Abroad.* Santa Ana, Calif.: Seven Locks Press, 1997.

Colvin, Donna, and Ralph Nader. *Good Works: A Guide to Careers in Social Change.* New York: Barricade Books, 1994.

Eberts, Marjorie, and Margaret Gisler. *Careers for Good Samaritans & Other Humanitarian Types.* Lincolnwood, Ill.: VGM Career Horizons, 1998.

Giese, Filomena, and Marilyn Borchardt. *Alternatives to the Peace Corps: A Directory of Third World & U.S. Volunteer Opportunities.* Oakland, Calif.: Food First Books, 1999.

Hamilton, Leslie, and Robert Tragert. *100 Best Nonprofits to Work for.* New York: ARCO Publishing, 1998.

Kilpatrick, Joseph, and Sanford Danziger. *Better Than Money Can Buy: The New Volunteers.* Winston-Salem, N.C.: Innersearch Publications, 1996.

Krannich, Ronald L., and Caryl Rae Krannich. *Jobs and Careers with Nonprofit Organizations: Profitable Opportunities with Nonprofits.* Manassas Park, Va.: Impact Publications, 1998.

Landes, Michael. *The Back Door Guide to Short Term Job Adventures: Internships, Extraordinary Experiences, Seasonal Jobs, Volunteering, Work Abroad.* Berkley, Calif.: Ten Speed Press, 1997.

McMillon, Bill, and Edward Asner. *Volunteer Vacations: Short-Term Adventures That Will Benefit You and Others.* Chicago, Ill.: Chicago Review Press, 1999.

CHECK IT OUT

American Council for Voluntary International Action
1717 Massachusetts Avenue NW, Suite 801
Washington, D.C. 20036
http://www.interaction.org

American Red Cross
18th and E Street NW
Washington, D.C. 20006
http://www.redcross.org

American Society of Association Executives
1575 I Street NW
Washington, D.C. 20005-1103
http://www.asaenet.org

Independent Charities of America
21 Tamal Boulevard, Suite 209
Corte Madera, Calif. 94925
http://www.independentcharities.org

Society for Nonprofit Organizations
6314 Odana Road, Suite 1
Madison, Wisconsin 53719-1141
http://www.danenet.org/snpo

GET ACQUAINTED

Douglas Allen,
International Relief Worker

CAREER PATH

CHILDHOOD ASPIRATION: To be a pilot.

FIRST JOB: Moving pallets around with a forklift in a warehouse in Peru.

CURRENT JOB: Manager of the international disaster relief unit of the American Red Cross.

AN INTERNATIONAL LIFE

Douglas Allen was born and spent his early years in South America, where his father worked as a mining engineer. It was an interesting start to a life that got even more interesting when Allen was about 10 or 11; that's when he "outgrew" the education provided where his family was living, and he was sent away to boarding school—first in Scotland and then in Massachusetts. He remembers that being 5,000 or 6,000 miles away from home was not a particularly fun experience, but he admits that he did get a great education in the process.

Allen's first encounter with an international relief agency was innocent enough. It was when he was nine, spending the summer in Canada, and earned a lifesaving swimming badge from the Red Cross. Later, while attending college in Florida, Allen got involved helping teach English to the children of migrant workers.

From the very beginning, Allen's career had an international flavor. His first job out of college was working the Latin American "desk" at a Canadian bank where he was responsible for merchant lending, and it required a lot of traveling. After that, he and some friends from business school started an import/export consulting business—more travel.

CAREER TO GO

Next up was a stint as director of development and public affairs for the Alexandria, Virginia, chapter of the American Red Cross. Hurricane Andrew hit while Allen was on the job, sending Allen and 14,000 volunteers to the rescue. Allen said that while a typical disaster requires about three weeks of help, this hurricane was so devastating that the project lasted more than a year.

After a couple of years with the Alexandria chapter, Allen moved on to the D.C. chapter. In 1991, he took his current job at the Red Cross national headquarters. Now he's in charge of a staff of 10 who work to prepare for, cope with, and manage all kinds of disaster relief efforts.

Since he's been on the job, he's been summoned to the scene of embassy bombings, tsunamis, earthquakes, hurricanes, floods, and mudslides. His work has taken him to virtually every corner of the world, including New Guinea, Colombia, Lebanon, Turkey, India, and Venezuela.

He says that regardless of the circumstances, the Red Cross starts each effort by conducting a needs assessment, a system that helps them figure out how to meet the basic needs of the most vulnerable people. Often that translates into targeting senior citizens and young children first and providing the most basic of resources—shelter, clean water, medicine, and food.

Allen says that sometimes the greatest challenge is not in having enough supplies but in finding ways to distribute them. That process can get tricky especially when trying to coordinate efforts with all kinds of other volunteers and organizations.

FACING TRAGEDY

No matter how you look at it, this is tough work. Yes, it is rewarding beyond words, but being confronted with so much tragedy is hard for anyone to deal with. Allen says that it helps to "keep the face of the beneficiaries right in front of you and you won't make many mistakes." He says one look at the grateful face of someone you are helping is all that it takes to put everything in perspective.

HELP FOR THE HELPERS

Allen cautions that this is not a job for people who simply want to travel and help people. His jet-setting lifestyle may sound glamorous to outsiders, but it's hard work, plain and simple. Relief work is an industry—with its own standards, vocabulary, and procedures, just like any other industry. It's not enough to see a need and try to fix it. In fact, some relief efforts are actually hampered by well-meaning volunteers who come to a place with unrealistic expectations.

Future relief workers would do well to start from the ground up, according to Allen. Volunteer with local nonprofit organizations. Take disaster training classes offered by Red Cross chapters all over the country. Get involved with a Red Cross disaster relief team. It will give you a better idea of what to expect and prepare you to provide help that really helps.

Interpreter

SKILL SET

✔ TRAVEL
✔ TALKING
✔ HISTORY

GO to a foreign country as an exchange student.

READ some of your favorite words in other languages on-line at http://www.freetranslation.com.

TRY learning a new language at school.

WHAT IS AN INTERPRETER?

Interpreters have to do two very important tasks at the same time: Talk and listen. An interpreter listens to words spoken in one language and verbally translates them into another language. This is different from a translator who translates written documents from one language into another.

There are two different types of interpretation. The first is simultaneous interpretation. This type of interpretation is done at a large meeting or event and requires some special equipment. The interpreter is usually in a booth with headphones and a microphone. As the interpreter hears the speaker through the headphones, he or she interprets the speaker's words simultaneously into the microphone. The trick is to keep up with the speaker. A good translator usually won't lag more than a sentence behind. Audience members can tune into the interpreter using headphones and hear in their native tongue what the speaker is saying.

The other kind of interpretation is consecutive interpretation in which the speaker and the interpreter take turns speaking. The interpreter listens and takes notes while the speaker talks and then gives an accurate interpretation of what has been said. Consecutive interpretation tends to be used with smaller groups or in more informal situations. For instance, an interpreter may be called on to escort foreign

dignitaries on sight-seeing trips or to interpret for business executives negotiating a contract.

Federal government agencies such as the State Department, FBI, and Agency for International Development, as well as the court system, the United Nations, and other international organizations employ quite a few interpreters and translators. Washington, D.C., and New York City are two hot spots where many interpreters find jobs.

Some interpreters specialize in a technical field such as science and medicine and may work for a private convention services firm. In these cases, a translator must be familiar with the professional jargon associated with each particular field.

Obviously, an interpreter has to be fluent in at least two languages. Interpreters with the United Nations are required to be fluent in at least three of their six official languages (Arabic, Chinese, English, French, Russian, and Spanish). In addition to knowing the language, an interpreter also needs a thorough understanding of both cultures. One way to learn about other cultures is to study them in world history classes, but the best way is actually to experience another culture by spending some time living in a foreign country.

Interpreting requires absolute concentration and can get a little stressful at times. It's fast paced, and there's always that chance that someone will use an unfamiliar word. It takes someone who can think on his or her feet. A translator can take the time to check dictionaries and other reference books for the correct answer, but an interpreter has only a split second to get it right.

A college degree in language or linguistics is required to become a professional interpreter. In some cases, an advanced degree in language and linguistics can be a good idea. Interpreting can be a rewarding career for someone who loves languages. Travel is one of the big perks because interpreters go where they are needed. They also get to meet interesting people from around the world, and if they're lucky, they sometimes witness history in the making.

TRY IT OUT

TALK IT UP

Get serious about learning foreign languages. Remember that the best interpreters know more than two. In addition to taking classes at school, utilize these on-line language resources to improve your fluency.

Start with About.com's Foreign Languages for Kids page at http://kidslangarts.about.com/kids/kidslangarts/cs/foreignlanguages/index.htm.

Try the Language Hub at http:www/cetrodftt.com/translate.htm for links to on-line courses and dictionaries for every language imaginable.

If you haven't had enough, finish up with the World Language Resource at http://www.geocities.com/virtual search/languages.html for the best on-line sites available for learning a foreign language. In addition to dictionaries, phrase books, and lessons, you will also find foreign language reading materials such as newspapers and magazines.

Oh, and just for fun, make the Travlang Word of the Day website at http://www.travlang.com/wordofday/ your home page, and each day you will hear a new word or a phrase translated into 50 different languages.

Use these resources to find out how to say some basic phrases in several different languages. Start with hello and work your way up to good-bye.

IT'S OPEN TO INTERPRETATION

Enlist the help of two friends. Get one friend to tell you a story. While you listen, paraphrase the story to your other friend, staying no more than one sentence behind. Can you listen and talk at the same time, or do you lose a sentence or two while you are relating the story? This activity will give you a taste of simultaneous interpretation without the burden of having to translate the story into another language.

PAL AROUND

Practice your foreign language skills by hooking up with an international pen pal. Not only will you get to converse with someone in another language, but you can also learn about his or her culture and customs. You might wind up with a lifelong friend—you just never know. About.com has some resources that can help you locate a pen pal at http://kidspenpals.about.com/kids/kidspenpals/cs/internationalpals/index.htm. If you have trouble understanding letters from your pen pal, go to http://www.freetranslation.com, type in the text, and have it translated free of charge.

OOPS!

Read some funny stories about translation boo-boos at Translation Terrors! At http://www.boslang.com/trans/stories.htm.

COOL CAREERS IN ANY LANGUAGE

Curl up with one of these books about foreign language careers.

Degalan, Julie, and Stephen E. Lambert. *Great Jobs for Foreign Language Majors.* Lincolnwood, Ill.: VGM Career Horizons, 1994.

Rivers, Wilga M., and Marguerite Duffy. *Opportunities in Foreign Language Careers.* Lincolnwood, Ill.: VGM Career Horizons, 1998.

Seelye, H. Ned, and J. Laurence Day. *Careers for Foreign Language Aficionados & Other Multilingual Types.* Lincolnwood, Ill.: VGM Career Horizons, 1991.

CHECK IT OUT

American Translators Association
225 Reinekers Lane, Suite 590
Alexandria, Virginia 22314
http://www.atanet.org

International Association of Conference Interpreters
10, avenue de Sécheron
CH-1202 Geneva, Switzerland
http://www.aiic.net

The National Association of Judiciary Interpreters and Translators
551 Fifth Avenue, Suite 3025
New York, New York 10176
http://www.najit.org

The Translators and Interpreters Guild
2007 North 15th Street, Suite 4
Arlington, Virginia 22201–2621
http://www.trans-interp-guild.org

GET ACQUAINTED

Deborah Joyce, Interpreter

CAREER PATH

CHILDHOOD ASPIRATION: To be a writer.

FIRST JOB: Apprentice pharmacist in high school.

CURRENT JOB: Self-employed interpreter and translator.

LOVE AT FIRST SOUND

Deborah Joyce wrote her first novel when she was 11 years old. It was quite a page-turner, featuring high fashion, travel, and celebrities. At the time, she was sure she was destined for a career as a great writer, but, when she was in junior high, she discovered something that she liked even better than writing—French. Joyce recalls that she immediately fell in love with the language and felt right at home with it from the very beginning.

French studies continued in high school, and when it came time for college, Joyce had a nice surprise in store. She tested so high on the French placement tests that she started out at the junior level and was able to graduate with both a bachelor's and master's degree at the same time—a coup de grâce in any language!

One of the highlights of her time in college was the year she spent in Switzerland. It was there that she learned one of the secrets to her success as a translator: How to read European handwriting. Apparently there is a difference and it helps to recognize it.

NEVER A DULL MOMENT

French has been the central theme in Joyce's career. It started with an enjoyable stint in with the French consulate in Chicago, followed by positions with a French telecommunications firm, a French airline, a waste management company with operations in French-speaking Canada, and an American toy company getting ready to expand its presence in Canada and Europe.

When family responsibilities made freelance work seem like a good idea, all this experience and Joyce's great contacts in the French business community made it a done deal. As a freelance translator and interpreter, Joyce says she never knows what to expect when the phone rings. So far, projects have included everything from translating important documents for a candy company to interpreting for officers from the French equivalent of the FBI while they chased down a white-collar criminal. Her work gets as varied as translating birth certificates and autopsy reports for the French consulate to working with a business specializing in bathroom fixtures and a French business trying to import fresh roses into America.

One time, when an art museum invited a curator from France to introduce a special exhibit of Monet's paintings, Joyce was asked to interpret a lecture that lasted an hour and a half on stage in front of 300 people. She says she was really glad she had the presence of mind to ask for a copy of the speech in advance because the speech mentioned every flower in Monet's garden using scientific terms—that's a task that would be hard enough to pronounce in English, let alone French! It took some homework, but Joyce managed to come through with flying colors.

At least twice a year, Joyce makes a point of scrounging up a week's worth of business in Paris. That city has become a home away from home for her.

A PERFECT FIT

Joyce is the first to admit that she never expected to be doing what she's doing. When she graduated from college, she thought her only option was to teach French, a job—it didn't take long to discover—that wasn't a good fit for her. She had no idea at the time that there would be so many interesting ways to put her talent to use.

Now a mother, Joyce encourages her children to find something they really like to do and get good at it. It's been a key to Joyce's success, and she believes it's a strategy that will work for anyone

Railroad Engineer

SKILL SET

✔ TRAVEL

✔ MATH

✔ ADVENTURE

WHAT IS A RAILROAD ENGINEER?

Railroad engineers are to trains what pilots are to planes; they run or operate trains carrying cargo or passengers from one place to another. Their biggest responsibility is to keep the train running safely. As "drivers" of the train, they work in the first car, or the engine car, of the train.

Before the whistle blows and the train rides off, the engineers are responsible for checking the train for mechanical troubles. Some minor repairs they handle themselves, but the big stuff is passed along to the engine shop. After completing a run, engineers check the locomotive again to make sure nothing went amiss during transit.

Engineers work closely with the train's conductor and the traffic control center to stay informed about oncoming trains, stops, and delays. Engineers have to run things by the book. There are rules and good reasons for each rule, and failure to follow the rules can cause huge problems. For instance, railroads use a very precise signaling system, which engineers must know and use to a tee. A good sense of direction and familiarity with railroad routes is often required for obvious reasons.

Trains run 24 hours a day, seven days a week, which often adds up to some pretty crazy schedules for railroad personnel. It's not unusual to work nights and some holidays. On the plus side, the work involves traveling to lots of different places. On the down side, it requires spending a lot of time away from home.

All railroads are unionized and regulated by the federal government, so an engineer's career path is well defined. An engineer must have a high school diploma and be at least 21 years old. Completing a formal engineer training program that includes classroom, simulator, and hands-on instruction is also required. Engineer positions are almost always filled with other railroad workers such as yard laborers or brakemen who work their way up the ranks. After completing training and passing an examination, an engineer receives a license.

At this point, the names of new engineers are placed on the "extra board" and are used as fill-ins for full-time engineers who are out sick or on vacation. This way, they ease into the position and get some good experience under their belts as they build up enough seniority to land a permanent engineer position.

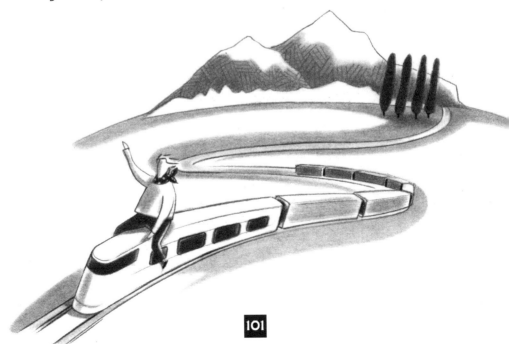

Railroad work is physically demanding, so engineers have to be healthy. Excellent eyesight and hearing are absolutely necessary. It helps to be mechanically inclined and have good eye-hand coordination. Federal law mandates that engineers be randomly tested for drugs and alcohol, so heavy drinkers and drug users need not apply.

Another railroad career to consider is conductor. Many people think of conductors as the person in a funny hat yelling "all aboard" and collecting tickets on a train. That's partly correct, but collecting tickets is just one of many of the conductor's responsibilities. Conductors are actually in charge of everything on the train; they are the bosses. They manage the rest of the train crew and make sure that the train leaves and gets where it's going on time. It's the conductor's job to signal the engineer to start and stop the train.

The conductor's job also starts before the train leaves the station. A conductor does a lot of planning before the trip starts and prepares reports after a trip is completed. On a passenger train, the conductor is responsible for the safety and comfort of all the passengers. The conductor knows the contents of every car on his or her train as well as the line-up of each car.

Conductors need a high school diploma, plenty of on-the-job training, and completion of a series of railroad exams. Completing a two-year associate's degree in railroad operations can't hurt an aspiring conductor's chances of promotion either. However, it is not unusual for this process to take a good 10 to 12 years. Many conductors start out as brakemen and work their way up. Working for the railroad can be a great way to see the country with regular visits to both exciting and not so exciting places.

TRY IT OUT

RUN THE RAILROAD

Get a feel for railroad life with 3-D Railroad Master, a railroading simulation game for your computer. You can download a demo copy of the program at http://www.abracadata.com/

html/index 99.html. 3-D Railroad Master allows you to build trains, define cargo, realistically control speed, braking, train direction, switching, horns, and lights. You can also control cargo loading and revenue tracking. Although 3-D Railroad Master is a game, it can give you a hint about all the details that go into making the railroad run.

RAILROAD BARONS

Visit your local hobby store for a mini-education in railroading. There you can see and operate scaled-down versions of actual train engines and cars and get a feel for track layout and switching systems. Collecting model trains is a hobby (that often becomes an obsession!) enjoyed by kids and adults, and it can be profitable if you make wise purchases and take care of your trains. Train or hobby shops are also a great resource for books and videos about trains and railroading.

I'VE BEEN SURFING ON THE RAILROAD

The Internet is loaded with information about railroading. Start with the sites listed here and enjoy the adventures they bring your way.

- ☼ Add some railroad slang to your vocabulary at http://www.fra.dot.gov/s/edu/school/curriculum/4-7/ slang4-7.html.
- ☼ Get a history lesson on the men who built the transcontinental railroad at http://www. bookmagazine.com/issue11/excerpt./shtml.
- ☼ Make plans to camp out at the Cyberspace World Railroad site at http://www.cwrr.com, where there are tons of links to railroad-related sites.
- ☼ Visit the site for *MOVIN Magazine,* a train publication at http://www.commerce.cn.ca/cnwebsite/ cnwebsite.nsf/Public/en_About MOVINMagazine.
- ☼ Trains Online at http://www2.trains.com/LeftFrame. html offers news, railroading links, and magazines on-line.

☀ The *Locomotive Engineer Newsletter* at http://www.ble.org/pr/newsletter/0400newsletter/ is published by the Brotherhood of Locomotive Engineers and has news and union information.

☀ Participate in railroad and model railroad forums at the Everything Railroading site at http://www.trainboard.com.

☀ Visit the Railroad Technology site at http://www.railway-technology.com for more technical railroad information.

☀ Read railroad stories and look at railroad art at http://www.railroadextra.com/page0002.html.

☀ Discover the world of Lionel trains at http://www.lionel.com.

SOME GOOD RAILROADING BOOKS

Grab your library card and check out some of these railroad books.

Armstrong, John. *Railroad: What It Is, What It Does.* New York: Simmons Boardman Publishing Co., 1990.

Foster, Gerald L. *A Field Guide to Trains of North America.* Boston, Mass.: Houghton, Mifflin Co., 1996.

Grant, John. *Great American Rail Journeys.* Guilford, Conn.: Globe Pequot Press, 2000.

Halberstadt, Hans. *Modern Diesel Locomotives.* Osceola, Wisc.: Motorbooks International, 1996.

Hay, William Walter. *Railroad Engineering.* New York: John Wiley & Sons, 1982.

Hiss, Tony, Mark Livingston, and Rogers E. M. Whitaker. *All Aboard with E.M. Frimbo: World's Greatest Railroad Buff.* Tokyo: Kodansha International, 1997.

Levinson, Nancy Smiler. *She's Been Working on the Railroad.* New York: Lodestar Books, 1997.

Riddell, Doug. *From the Cab: Stories from a Locomotive Engineer.* Pasadena, Calif.: Pentrex, 1999.

Tufnell, Robert. *The New Illustrated Encyclopedia of Railroad Locomotives.* New York: Book Sales, 2000.

CHECK IT OUT

American Short Line and Regional Railroad Association
1120 G Street NW, Suite 520
Washington, D.C. 20005-3889
http://www.aslrra.org/

Association of American Railroads
50 F Street NW
Washington, D.C. 20001-1564
http://www.aar.org

Brotherhood of Locomotive Engineers
1370 Ontario Street, Mezzanine
Cleveland, Ohio 44113-1702
http://www.ble.org

GET ACQUAINTED

Clyde George,
Railroad Engineer

CAREER PATH

CHILDHOOD ASPIRATION: To be a grown-up.

FIRST JOB: Busboy at a bowling alley.

CURRENT JOB: Railroad engineer.

THREE GENERATIONS OF RAILROADING

Clyde George has been working on the railroad for thirty years. He is the third generation of his family to work on the railroad. His grandfather was a "hogger" (railroad slang for an engineer), and his dad was a conductor.

His life's ambition as a child was to be a grown-up because he suspected that being an adult was far more interesting than being a kid. His career aspirations changed frequently and included being a fireman, policeman, doctor, and lawyer. Now that he's a grown-up, he admits that he'd like another shot at being a kid!

George started out as a brakeman before being promoted to conductor, then engineer. It took him about six years of hard work to land the coveted engineer job.

ALL DAY, EVERY DAY

George is on call 24 hours a day, seven days a week. When a call comes in from the train station, he's got just an hour and a half to get there—day or night. That's just enough time to pack some clothes and throw some food together.

Once he gets there, he and the conductor go over all the details of the trip. They discuss what the train will be transporting, the kinds of railroad cars attached to the train, and the travel route. A train can include a combination of boxcars filled with food, clothing, or other commodities; tank cars filled with liquids; flat cars; and engines. George controls all the cars from the lead engine.

DEFYING GRAVITY

George's usual run is from Bakersfield, California, to Colton or Los Angeles, California. He travels across the Tehachapi Mountains and through the Mojave Desert. George manipulates the controls of his engine to safely transport huge amounts of weight down steep grades, a feat he likens to defying gravity.

He yards (parks) the train in a rail yard, where the yard crew then switches the cars into other yard tracks; eventually these cars become part of other trains. The goods he moves make their way across the nation and into stores.

ONE PART BUMMER, ONE PART COOL

For George, the worst part of his job is the time away from home and family. He feels he has often sacrificed important relationships because of his work. On the other hand, he loves the sense of accomplishment he gets after completing a run, and he has enjoyed working with some really interesting people. His favorite part of being an engineer is waving to folks as his train goes by.

THREE WORDS TO THE WISE

Stay in school! That's what he advises kids to do. George went to college for a few years but never finished; to this day, he wishes he had. He thinks an education is even more important now than when he was coming up the ranks.

George also suggests that job seekers find something fun to do that they can enjoy for the long haul. Another thing he's learned is that serving others gives a person a sense of fulfillment that is hard to find any other way.

Regional Sales Manager

SKILL SET

✔ TRAVEL

✔ TALKING

✔ MONEY

GO with your parents the next time they make a major purchase such as a car or kitchen appliance and watch the sales team in action.

READ *The One-Minute Sales Person* by Spencer Johnson (Berkeley, Calif.: Berkeley Publishing Group, 1997).

TRY selling the most for your school's next fund-raiser.

WHAT IS A REGIONAL SALES MANAGER?

What do a submarine, a truckload of chocolate, a computer network, and a prescription drug have in common? Salespeople sold these very different products to customers as different as the products. Foreign governments, grocery stores, businesses of all kinds, and hospitals are just a few of the customers visited by regional sales managers every day.

Officially speaking, a regional sales manager develops and implements strategies for certain products within a specified region or territory. Depending on the company, a region could be a county, state, group of states, country, or an entire continent.

First and foremost, a regional sales manager is a salesperson. No matter what other duties might be included in a particular job description, the main responsibility of regional sales managers is to sell products—either directly by making sales calls on their own or indirectly by managing a sales force. Regional salespeople tend to work their way up through the ranks of a sales department by proving themselves with exceptional performance and results.

Regional sales managers have to know their product line, and it really helps to believe in it too. It's just easier to sell something that you take pride in. Their job is to communicate the features and benefits of their product line to customers most likely to want or need the products. The closer the link between carefully targeted customers and the product, the more likely the sale. Good sales managers know where to find likely customers and know how to close the deal.

A regional sales manager is often responsible for recruiting, hiring, training, and managing a winning sales staff. Depending on the company, the staff could include a few people or a few hundred people.

Training can make the difference between a mediocre sales team and a magnificent one. That's why a regional sales manager tends to make training a high priority. The manager's role in this process can include developing training programs and materials. It absolutely includes communicating goals and keeping the sales team motivated. Since sales managers' salaries are usually based at least in part on the successful sales of their staff, there's a strong incentive to keep racking up those sales.

Travel can take up to 50 percent of a regional sales manager's time. Visiting new customers, introducing new products, presenting sales proposals, checking up on staff, or attending trade shows are all good reasons for a regional sales manager to hit the road.

Communication is the name of the game for salespeople. That goes double for regional sales managers. People who succeed in this field understand what makes people tick. Regional sales managers are not only good talkers but good writers as well. They write sales plans, reports, evaluations, proposals, and sometimes even sales and marketing materials.

It generally takes a good five years of solid selling experience to become eligible for a regional sales management position. A college degree is usually required and some companies like their managers to have an MBA. As far as majors go, business is a good bet. Some colleges offer sales and marketing degrees, which are also good. Some sales jobs require specialized training. For example, a pre-med or science degree might be helpful to a pharmaceutical salesperson. A computer science degree might give a leg up to someone wishes to sell computer products or network services.

A career in sales can be a good way to connect a career with personal interests. For example, someone who loves sports might think about selling sporting goods. Bookworms might check into representing a publisher.

TRY IT OUT!

DO SOME RESEARCH

Think about a product you like. It can be anything: clothes, food, airplanes, horses. Anything! Spend some time just thinking about how the product gets to the end user. Somebody makes it, grows it, or breeds it. Does that person sell directly to the consumer or does it go through a middleman like a store? Now, go on-line and use a search engine such as Yahoo! or Lycos to see if you can find out more about the process. If it's planes you're interested in, enter words such as "airplane sales" or "airplane manufacturer." Be creative and find out who sells what to whom and how.

WHAT'S YOUR STRATEGY?

You are the regional sales manager for Shaggy's Custom Surf Boards. Your region is made up of California, Hawaii, and the Caribbean Islands. Your job is to get your company's boards into all 500 surf shops in your region. Develop a sales strategy to get the job done. Answer these questions:

- To whom am I selling?
- What is the best way to reach them? By phone? Personal visit?
- What kind of materials will I need?
- How many employees will I need?
- What kinds of qualities do they need?
- How will I train them?

Once you have the answers to all these questions and any others that you think of, write up a report.

SELL YOURSELF!

Get some incredible sales experience and earn some cold hard cash by starting your own business. You can go the traditional route and mow lawns, baby-sit, or wash cars. Or, if you're the more creative type, you might come up with a product such as tie-dyed T-shirts that you can sell. No matter which route you choose, do some planning and get out there and sell yourself. Fleet Kids has all the information you will need to start a business including what equipment and supplies you will need. Check it out at http://headbone.go.com/fleet/.

- Entrepreneurial-minded girls can find out more about running their own business at Independent Mean's site at http://www.independentmeans.com. They even have camps that teach girls to earn an income of their own.
- Read *Sales & Marketing Management Magazine* on-line at http://www.salesandmarketing.com.

☼ Check out sales resources at http://www.sales.com.
☼ Find out everything you ever wanted to know about sales at *SalesDoctors Magazine* at http://www.salesdoctors.com/free/free068.htm.
☼ SalesLinks at http://www.saleslinks.com is loaded with information, tools, resources and links for professional sellers.
☼ Learn how to close a sale at http://209.241.14.8/fmpro?-db=library.fp5&-format=fulltext1.htm&Record=H6395&-find.
☼ Experts share five ways not to blow a sale at http://www.inc.com/incmagazine/article/0,,ART1805,00.html.

THE BUSINESS OF BOOKS

Sit down with one of these books about sales and sales management.

———————————

Alessandra, Tony, John Monoky, and Gregg Baron. *The Sales Manager's Idea-A-Day Guide: 250 Ways to Manage and Motivate a Winning Sales Team—Every Selling Day of the Year.* Palm Beach Gardens, Fl.: Dartnell Corp., 1996.

Brown, Ronald. *From Selling to Managing: Guidelines for the First-Time Sales Manager.* New York: AMACOM, 1990.

Davis, Kevin, and Kenneth H. Blanchard. *Getting into Your Customer's Head: The Eight Roles of Customer-Focused Selling.* New York: Times Books, 1996.

Farr, J. Michael. *America's Top Office Management, Sales & Professional Jobs: Good Jobs That Offer Advancement & Excellent Pay.* Indianapolis: JIST Works, 1996.

Schiffman, Stephan. *The 25 Sales Habits of Highly Successful Salespeople.* Holbrook, Mass.: Adams Media Corporation, 1994.

Tracy, Brian. *Advanced Selling Strategies: The Proven System of Sales Ideas, Methods, and Techniques Used by Top Salespeople.* New York: Fireside, 1996.

Wilner, Jack D. *Seven Secrets to Successful Sales Management: The Sales Manager's Manual.* Boca Raton, Fla.: CRC Press, 1997.

———————————

CHECK IT OUT

National Association of Sales Professionals
8300 North Hayden Road, Suite 207
Scottsdale, Arizona 85258
http://www.nasp.com

National Confectionery Sales Association
10225 Berea Road, Suite B
Cleveland, Ohio 44102
http://www.candyhalloffame.com/ncsa

Sales & Marketing Executives International
P.O. Box 1390
Sumas, Washington 98295-1390
http://www.smei.org

GET ACQUAINTED

Mike Hamburger,
Regional Sales Manager

CAREER PATH

CHILDHOOD ASPIRATION: To be a fireman.

FIRST JOB: Stockboy in the hardware section of a department store.

CURRENT JOB: Director of specialty sales for Ghirardelli Chocolate Company.

FOLLOWING IN DAD'S FOOTSTEPS

When Mike Hamburger was a child, he fantasized about being a fireman and riding around town on the back of a shiny, red fire truck. As he got older, however, even the excitement of the sirens didn't measure up to Hamburger's nominee for the coolest guy in the world—his dad. His dad also had a pretty cool job as a food distributor with access to all kinds of candies and gourmet foods.

College offered Hamburger a chance to get ready to join his father's business. Four years later, with a degree in marketing and management and a company car, Hamburger was visiting major grocery chains and specialty stores throughout the northwestern part of the country. The job required him to be in certain places at certain times, and Hamburger credits the experience with helping him grow up.

A sad turn of events changed Hamburger's career track: His father died and Hamburger ended up selling the business to a competitor. He tried staying with the company for a while but it just wasn't the same.

COFFEE, CHOCOLATES, AND SNUFF LIKE THAT

Before Hamburger joined his present employer, he helped a friend launch a business packaging and selling a safe alternative to chewing tobacco made out of a concoction of mint leaves and sugar. He also helped "clean up" a company specializing in supplying whole bean coffee to venture capitalists.

By now, Hamburger had proven himself an effective sales director so it wasn't hard to find another job. This time it was with Ghirardelli (pronounced gear-ar-delly), a gourmet chocolate company. His first position was as midwest regional sales manager, which made him responsible for covering grocery chains and specialty markets in 20 states. At the time, the company had very few clients in the region, so Hamburger figured there was nowhere to go but up. Up was exactly where sales levels went over the next four years—from under $1 million in sales to more than 4.5 million.

When Hamburger asked to be transferred back to his home state of Oregon, Ghirardelli was only too happy to accommodate him. There he took over a smaller market but cranked sales up from $1 million to $6 million in just three years. Hamburger was named sales manager of the year in 1998 for his efforts.

A CHOCOLATE-COVERED CAREER

Now Hamburger is the national accounts manager in charge of special markets, which means his territory is anywhere you see chocolate besides grocery stores and drug stores. His team brings in about $28 million in sales each year (that's a LOT of chocolate).

Travel has been a big part of Hamburger's career from day one. If he's not jetting off to Dallas or Minneapolis, it's Alaska or Atlanta. At least a part of every week is spent in the air.

At one point, Hamburger recalls being on the road so much that one morning, when he woke up in yet another identical hotel room, he had to call the front desk to figure out where he was! Nowadays, Hamburger varies the types of hotels he stays in to help keep things straight.

GOOD RELATIONSHIPS

Hamburger's father told him that there are two things people can't take from you: your education and your reputation. It's advice that he's put to use throughout his career. In this line of work, relationships are everything. Hamburger says you really get to know your clients. They need to be sure that you know what you're doing and that you'll do what you'll say you'll do. Maybe a secret of Hamburger's success is that meeting new people every day is his favorite part of the job. Of course, working for a chocolate company has other perks. Access to all that great chocolate is pretty nice too!

Tour Guide

TAKE A TRIP!

SKILL SET

✔ TRAVEL

✔ TALKING

✔ ADVENTURE

SHORTCUTS

GO "camp out" in the travel section of a big bookstore and explore some of the exciting and exotic places to visit.

READ *Learning Adventures Around the World* by Peter Greenberg (Princeton, N.J.: Peterson's, 1997) for ideas on expanding your horizons.

TRY guiding your friends on a hike or tour of a local historical site.

WHAT IS A TOUR GUIDE?

If you could spend your time doing anything, what would you do? Would it be an outdoor activity like hiking or mountain biking? Are you crazy about art? Maybe it's visiting a special place, like Paris. Maybe it's shopping or just traveling to new places around the world. Many people have turned passions just like these into successful careers as tour guides. Tour guides organize trips and tours and accompany people who are visiting a location or an attraction. They provide information, assistance, and, with a little luck, a dash of excitement.

Tour guides generally specialize in a certain place or a type of activity. Some specialize in destinations such as Hawaii, Europe, or South America. Others specialize in an activity such as white-water rafting, hiking, or bicycling. Another type of specialization has to do with different groups of people—senior citizens, youth, singles, professional associations, or families with young children. Yet another type of tour guide focuses on a specific attraction such as a museum or historical site. This type of tour guide is often a history buff and enjoys re-creating life as it once was.

Above all, tour guides are experts. The very nature of their work requires that they know at least a little more than the average person about their area of specialization. For instance, guides who lead guests on adventure bicycling tours must know the region and various cycling routes like the back of their hands. They must point out places of historical interest as well as all the best restaurants and stores in town. Expertise in bicycling and maintenance is a given since someone's got to know how to fix the inevitable flat tires! Guides leading more challenging trips such as white-water rafting or mountain climbing adventures must also be able to teach guests the ins and outs of the activity as well as be prepared to keep guests safe in all kinds of wild situations.

A guide at a historical site will be extremely knowledgeable about the events that took place there. She will be able to tell interesting stories that transport her visitors back in time and make historical events come alive.

In the same way, a tour guide leading a shopping trip has connections with the best shops in town, knows where to find bargains, and manages to take his guests "off the beaten path" to unusual or particularly exquisite shops. Anyone can find the local Wal-Mart but a special tour guide creates a shopping experience that tourists would be hard pressed to duplicate on their own.

Details are the common factor for all types of tour guides, and there are plenty of them. Attention to details often starts long before a tour begins. Tour guides spend time planning events, advertising them, and keeping track of reservations. The details continue nonstop during the tour itself. Keeping guests on track with a daily schedule and making sure everyone gets to the next stop safely is part of the job. Tour guides also make sure that appropriate accommodations are lined up, and they take care of "comfort" details such as overnight accommodations, transportation, meals, and help with luggage. For the duration of a tour, a tour guide is at the group's beck and call to answer questions, give aid in emergencies, and keep everyone happy.

There are tour guides and there are TOUR GUIDES! The former is someone who guides tours, and the latter is someone who turns every tour into a memorable and enjoyable experience. Good tour guides can make any subject matter come alive. They have lots of interesting stories and anecdotes to share, and they truly enjoy working with people. Let's face it. Sightseeing can get pretty boring sometimes; for instance, what's so exciting about visiting a dark and dreary old castle? But the right tour guide can transport guests back in history so completely that they expect to run into a knight in shining armor or damsel in distress at any moment.

The skills required to be a tour guide are as varied as the types of tours available. A guide leading kayak trips probably wouldn't find an extensive knowledge of art terribly useful, but physical strength and endurance as well as experience in rough water would be extremely useful. In the same vein, a tour guide at an art museum wouldn't be required to know how to do an Eskimo roll. This is one profession in which there's lots of room to blend passion and talents with career opportunities.

A tour guide has to be comfortable speaking in front of people. Leadership qualities are also important because the tour guide often has to "take charge." A college degree is an asset for a tour guide. Majors to think about are art, history, public relations, and hospitality. A two- or four-year program in tourism is also worth considering.

The really cool thing about being a tour guide is that it combines work with play. Tour guides get paid for doing something they love to do and often get free travel opportunities to boot.

TRY IT OUT

DON'T KNOW MUCH ABOUT HISTORY

Visit the National Register of Historic Places on-line at http://www.cr.nps.gov/nr/index.htm. Use their National Register Research and look for a historic site that's near your home. Pick a site and use the research feature to find photographs, maps, descriptions, and information about its history. Use the Web and library to find out more about the site you chose.

When you have enough information, put together a presentation highlighting the interesting things you learned. Get some friends together and accompany them on a tour of your site. Share your presentation with them. If you're brave enough, ask them for feedback about your performance after your'e done.

GET ORGANIZED!

Download Tour Organizer Lite, free software used for planning tours, at http://www.grouptour.com/planning/index.html. Use this software as you plan a tour to the destination of your choice. Pick a location and a place to stay. Find some restaurants and attractions. The search engine at http://www.grouptour.com will allow you to search for restaurants, attractions, and lodging that cater to tour groups. Do some research so you are familiar with the location and attractions.

SURFIN' FOR ADVENTURE

See for yourself all the different kinds of tours that are offered by doing a search on the Internet. Use Yahoo!'s search engine and enter these keywords:

💡 "tours"
💡 "adventure tours"
💡 "tour guides"

Just visiting those sites will take a while. Here are some others to visit when you're done.

💡 Read bios of some of the tour guides that work for Bicycle Adventures at http://www.bicycleadventures. com/who/guides2.html.
💡 Get the scoop on the two-week intensive training courses offered by the International Tour Management Institute at http://www.itmitourtraining. com/html/index2.html.
💡 Find a list of World Tourism Organization Education and Training Centers at http://www.world-tourism.org, http://www.humberc.on.ca/~ftcal/courses/eco_206.htm, and http://www.coronacollege.com/guide.htm.
💡 Link to interesting articles about Outside Expeditions at http://www.getoutside.com/media.shtml.

BOOK TOURS

Take a tour of your favorite library and check out some of these books on tour guiding.

Braidwood, Barbara, Susan M. Boyce, and Richard Cropp. *Start and Run a Profitable Tour Guiding Business.* Bellingham, Wash.: Self-Counsel Press, 2000.

Gaylord, Terri, and Marc Mancini, Ph.D. *Conducting Tours: A Practical Guide.* Albany, N.Y.: Delmar Publishers, 2000.

Pond, Kathleen Lingle. *The Professional Guide: Dynamics of Tour Guiding.* New York: John Wiley & Sons, 1992.

CHECK IT OUT

Adventure Travel Society
228 North F Street
Salida, Colorado 81201
http://www.adventuretravel.com

National Tour Association
546 East Main Street
Lexington, Kentucky 40596
http://www.ntaonline.com

U.S. Tour Operators Association
340 Madison Avenue, Suite 1522
New York, New York 10173
http://www.ustoa.com

World Tourism Organization
Capitan Haya 42
28020 Madrid, Spain
http://www.world-tourism.org

GET ACQUAINTED

Shelley Gumucio, Tour Guide

CAREER PATH

CHILDHOOD ASPIRATION: To be a teacher, dancer, or dolphin.

FIRST JOB: Lifeguard at a community pool.

CURRENT JOB: Trip leader for Backroads Bicycle Company.

FLIPPER FANTASIES

No, that wasn't a misprint; as a child, Shelley Gumucio really did want to be a dolphin when she grew up. She realized pretty early that she couldn't make a living "being a dolphin," so she decided that being a lifeguard was the next best thing. She loves swimming and being in the water, so it was a great first job for her.

Gumucio majored in communications at Boston College, and her first full-time job was in the human resources department at Harvard. Now she's traded in the corporate world for the great outdoors. Her job is to lead week-long biking, hiking, and multisport vacations. Since her employer offers trips to 36 different countries, the job comes with lots of adventure and plenty of travel.

FRIENDLY ADVICE

One of Backroad's satisfied customers, who also happened to be a coworker with Gumucio, inspired her job change. He'd gone on a trip to Costa Rica and came back convinced that—with Gumucio's love of the outdoors, swimming, biking, and running—she'd make an awesome trip leader. This friend convinced her to apply for a job. After a rigorous application and interviewing process, Gumucio was hired. That's in spite of some pretty tough competition, since Backroads receives nearly 3,000 applications every year and hires only about 65 people.

So far, Gumucio has led biking trips in Nantucket, Martha's Vineyard, and northern California wine country. She has also led hiking trips in Bryce and Zion National Parks and walking, biking, and sea kayaking trips in Georgia and South Carolina. She will be leading trips in Belize and Hawaii soon.

EARLY TO BED, EARLY TO RISE

It's up with the sun (and often before) for Gumucio. She typically wakes up in a wonderfully charming inn and gets everything ready for her group. She inspects everyone's bikes, fills the tires, and puts out water, Gatorade, snacks, and lunch stuff for the guests to pack before they take off. Making tuna sandwiches at six in the morning isn't exactly Gumucio's favorite part of the day, but she realizes that other aspects of her job more than make up for it.

After a hearty home-cooked breakfast at the inn, Gumucio gives a 10-minute "route rap" in which she explains the highlights of the upcoming ride. She includes some history of the area, flora and fauna, good picnic spots, and fun places to stop and shop. She makes sure to remind her group about biking safely and staying hydrated. By 9:00 A.M., the group is off and riding, ready to enjoy a 45-mile, off-the-beaten-path kind of trip. During the ride, Gumucio's job is to keep tabs on everyone, take photos, fix flats, and make sure everyone is having a good time.

RIDE-BY SQUIRTER

Gumucio carries a first aid kit, sunscreen, and provisions just in case one of the guests needs some help. She also packs a squirt gun and enjoys using it on other riders when they least expect it. It's a little touch that can perk things up when people start getting hot and tired.

Mind you, however, this job is not about baby-sitting people on bikes. A big part of Gumucio's job is sharing interesting aspects of the region with her guests. Before each trip, she has to learn about the area's history, people, culture, traditions, plants, and animals so she can entertain and educate her guests with all kinds of fascinating information.

CHOCOLATE THERAPY

Each ride ends at another nice hotel or inn where there's more work waiting for Gumucio. She makes sure that all the room arrangements are settled, reconfirms dinner reservations, leaves schedules for the next day in each guest's room, and arranges for help with getting the luggage into the van the next morning. Then it's time to freshen up for a gourmet meal with the guests. Gumucio admits that after a long ride there's nothing quite like a big piece of chocolate cake to replenish her energy and get her ready for a good night's rest!

KNOW THYSELF

Gumucio thinks it's a good idea for young people to spend some time figuring out what kind of things they really enjoy doing before settling on a career. She says to think about what you choose to do with your free time and what activities you do again and again. Also, ask other people to tell you what your strengths are. She feels the answers to those questions will help you find a career you'll be happy with.

Travel Agent

SKILL SET

✔ TRAVEL

✔ TALKING

✔ COMPUTERS

GO visit a travel agency. Leaf through travel brochures on exciting locales.

READ a Frommer's travel guide on a location that interests you.

TRY taking a foreign language at school.

WHAT IS A TRAVEL AGENT?

You've just come back from a relaxing lunch, and your telephone rings. You are expecting a potential customer looking to book a fabulous vacation. Instead it is an irate customer calling from Timbuktu. The hotel where you sent him has no record of a reservation ever being made, and there are no vacancies. Your customer is in a strange place with no place to stay and is furious with you! Can you keep your cool and find a way out of a horrible situation (which may or may not be your fault)? Can you calm your customer down, take some responsibility for the problem (even though it may not be your fault), and restore his faith in you (because you want him to book trips with you again)? If not, don't read any further because this scenario and others like it are a regular part of a travel agent's job. A travel agent makes all kinds of travel arrangements for all kinds of clients.

A lot of detail work goes into planning the perfect vacation. Travel agents have to be familiar with all sorts of different destinations and travel packages. Some agents specialize in certain types of trips (such as cruises) or specific regions of the world (such as Europe). When a potential customer comes in, the travel agent has to listen to find out exactly what kind of trip the customer wants. Is it a honeymoon, a business trip, or a family vacation? What is the customer's budget? Can she afford first class all the way or does she need to pinch her pennies?

Some customers know exactly where they want to go, while others look to their travel agent for a lot of guidance in selecting just the right trip. The agent uses special computer programs as well as travel savvy to find the best options for the customer. This process often involves some give and take as the agent works with the client to work out all the kinks and get all the details straight.

Next comes actually booking the trip, which is, after all, the travel agent's goal in the whole process. This step is especially important since commissions from airlines, hotels, rental car agencies, and cruise lines is how travel agents get paid.

Once a trip has been purchased, the travel agent goes about the business of making it happen. This involves making airline and hotel reservations, booking rental cars and making arrangements for tours, sightseeing, and recreational activities. When international travel is involved, the travel agent may walk clients through the process of obtaining a passport and provide information about customs regulations and currency exchange rates. A good travel agent is also a good source of tips on where to eat and what to see in places all over the world.

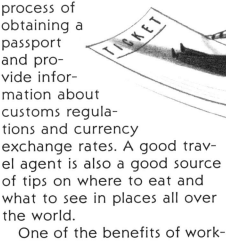

One of the benefits of working as a travel agent is discounted travel. Also, agents sometimes get to take FAM

(familiarization) trips at little cost to them. These trips allow them to familiarize themselves with different destinations. They check out hotels and attractions so they can better sell the destination to their customers.

It is possible to get an entry-level job, such as receptionist, at a travel agency and receive on-the-job training to become an agent. However, most agencies require some college or vocational training. Some specialized travel agent training programs take just six to 12 weeks to complete. Some schools also offer two- or four-year degrees in travel and tourism.

Most travel agents work for established agencies. Some eventually start their own agencies. Others work for a large business and make travel arrangements for people employed there. New computer technology has also opened up some interesting possibilities for home-based travel agents. Some of the most successful agents specialize in special kinds of trips or offer full-service tours.

TRY IT OUT

YOU'RE HIRED!

Help! The local travel agency is swamped. They need some help getting through the peak travel season, and you're the person for the job. Here's the skinny on your first client: A family of four wants to take a trip to Honolulu, Hawaii, for two weeks in January. Use the following websites to find them the best airfares and hotel and car rental deals.

Airlines
- ☀ Delta at http://www.delta.com
- ☀ United Airlines at http://www.united.com
- ☀ American Airlines at http://www.aa.com

Hotels
- ☀ Hilton Hotels at http://www.hilton.com
- ☀ Holiday Inn at http://www.basshotels.com/holiday-inn
- ☀ Marriott Hotels at http://www.marriott.com

Car Rental
  ☀ Alamo at http://www1.goalamo.com
  ☀ Budget at http://drivebudget.com
  ☀ Avis at http://www.avis.com

Play around with the arrival and departure dates and see if that affects the price. Visit Yahoo!'s travel guide for Honolulu at http://travel.yahoo.com/t/North_America/United_States/ Hawaii/Honolulu/ for sightseeing information and tourist attractions. Then prepare a summary for a budget trip, mid-priced trip, and luxury trip including places to go and things to see.

PICK A LOCATION, ANY LOCATION
Select a travel destination that seems exciting to you and research it thoroughly. Start at http://dmoz.org/recreation/ travel. Find out everything you can about the location including how you get there, what hotels are there, what makes it special, what the currency exchange rate is, and seasonal weather conditions. Use the information you gather to make a travel brochure that sells that destination.

CYBER DESTINATIONS
There are some great travel sites on the web. Take a look at these to get started.

  ☀ Check out Travel Zoo's guide to travel sales and specials at http://www.travelzoo.com.
  ☀ Find travel guides for lots of different locations at http://www.bootsnall.com.
  ☀ The Intrepid Traveler at http://www.intrepidtraveler. com is an informative and educational site for those who want to make travel an integral part of life.
  ☀ Visit http://www.traveltrade.com, the business paper of the travel industry. It has news of interest to travel agents.
  ☀ Find a list of tools for travel agents at The Fam Connection at http://www.redshift.com/~talisman/ publications.html.

☿ Travel Weekly Crossroads at http://www.twcrossroads. com is an on-line magazine for travel professionals.
☿ Check out the deals travel agents are getting on family trips at http://www.redshift.com/talisman/ FamConnection.html.

BOOK A TRIP TO THE LIBRARY

Visit the library and get the inside scope on a career as a travel agent. Start with a handful of these books.

Burgan, Michael. *Travel Agent (Career Exploration)*. Mankato, Minn.: Capstone Press, 2000.

Gee, Chuck Y., Kevin B. Boberg, James G. Makens, and Dexter J. L. Choy. *Professional Travel Agency Management*. Englewood Cliffs, N.J.: Prentice Hall, 1990.

Gregory, Aryear. *The Travel Agent: Dealer in Dreams*. Englewood Cliffs, N.J.: Prentice Hall College Division, 1992.

Hawks, John. *Career Opportunities in Travel and Tourism*. New York: Facts On File, 1996.

Meadows, Carl. *How to Organize Group Travel for Fun and Profit: Make Money, Travel for Fun, Make New Friends, Live the Good Life!* Littleton, Colo.: ETC Publishing Inc., 2000.

Monaghan, Kelly. *Home-Based Travel Agent: How to Cash in on the Exciting New World of Travel Marketing*. New York: Intrepid Traveler, 1999.

Payette, Douglas A. *So You Want to Be a Travel Agent: An Introduction to Domestic Travel*. Upper Saddle River, N.J.: Prentice Hall, 1994.

Ramsey, Dan. *The Upstart Guide to Owning and Managing a Travel Service*. Dover, N.H.: Upstart Publishing Company, 1995.

Todd, Ginger, and Susan Rice. *Travel Perspectives: A Guide to Becoming a Travel Agent*. Albany, N.Y.: Delmar Publishing, 1995.

CHECK IT OUT

American Society of Travel Agents
1101 King Street, Suite 200
Alexandria, Virginia 22314
http://www.astanet.com

The Institute of Certified Travel Agents
148 Linden Street
P.O. Box 812059
Wellesley, Massachusetts 02181-0012
http://www.icta.com

Travel Industry Association of America
New York Avenue NW, Suite 450
Washington, D.C. 20005
http://www.tia.org

GET ACQUAINTED

Michelle Abrate,
Travel Agent

CAREER PATH

CHILDHOOD ASPIRATION: To be an attorney.

FIRST JOB: Working in a dress shop.

CURRENT JOB: President of Armstrong & Hedges, purveyors of fine travel.

WHEN A VACATION IS NOT A VACATION

Michelle Abrate had a hero when she was younger: It was Gladys Towles Root, a prominent trial lawyer in Los Angeles.

She wanted to grow up to be just like her. But that was before an extended trip to Europe sparked her love of art and travel.

She majored in art history, graduated, and worked briefly for an art gallery, but she soon found herself right smack in the middle of an economic recession when cushy art jobs were few and far between. Abrate admits she's among those people who tend to give more thought to making their Christmas card list than to their career path, so she didn't have any overwhelming ambitions in the art world. She did, however, find it necessary to do something to pay the bills, so she took a job with a travel company specializing in carriage trade, which means most of the customers were wealthy.

There she enjoyed the best sides of travel and honed her skills in sales and building relationships. The travel was plentiful and luxurious, and the people were interesting. By the time Abrate left that agency to manage another one, the travel bug had bitten and she was hooked.

ADVENTURES IN TRAVEL

With more than 20 years experience in the travel industry, Abrate's career continues to blossom in exciting ways. When it comes to travel agencies, she's done it all—managed them, set up shop as an independent agent, worked as a "temp" in 60 different offices in just a three-year time span, and directed marketing activities for an upscale leisure travel business. She was even elected president of a professional association for travel agents, which gave her an opportunity to travel all over the world speaking about her profession.

All this experience helped Abrate eventually earn the distinction of certified travel consultant and instructor. This rigorous training credential is roughly the equivalent of earning a master's degree. Not a bad achievement for someone who never attended travel school!

One thing that Abrate noticed in all this is that smaller agencies with a reputation for doing a certain kind of travel seemed to enjoy a higher degree of success than those that

do a little bit of everything. She also discovered an area of travel that wasn't getting much attention from other agencies—that of providing special travel opportunities just for women.

A TRIP OF A LIFETIME

Abrate is now president of a company that specializes in arranging once-in-a-lifetime trips for women. Whether it's a daffodil festival in Nantucket, a fully guided mother/daughter tour of Paris and Provence, or a cottage garden tour in England, Abrate's trips pull out all the stops. Through great contacts and lots of research, Abrate finds those out-of-the-way places and provides the extra touches that make each trip a memory to cherish.

Abrate says staging events like these takes more organization skills than you could imagine. It's a good thing that she is an astute multitasker who can juggle lots of projects at once. She says it's not unusual to be making some sort of contact with all seven continents in one day!

THINGS YOU DON'T LEARN IN TRAVEL SCHOOL

Making it in this business requires more than a love of travel, according to Abrate. There's a lot to learn and dues to pay along the way. She also says that you don't learn some of the most important lessons in travel school. For instance, she sees three skills as critical to success: sales savvy, marketing muscle, and negotiating know-how. Top that off with an ability to present yourself in a professional manner, and you've got that extra edge to write your own ticket as a travel agent.

BY THE WAY

You are invited to visit Abrate's website at http://www. teagardentravel.com to learn about her business for yourself.

Truck Driver

WHAT IS A TRUCK DRIVER?

Have you ever thought about how all the food you eat, the clothes you wear, the furniture you sit on, and your favorite pair of tennis shoes got to your hometown? Chances are that most of those things were grown or manufactured some-where else and got to you courtesy of a truck driver.

Simply put, a truck driver picks up and delivers goods. The kinds of goods they deliver vary greatly; truck drivers haul anything and everything including produce, furniture, auto-mobiles, manufactured homes, gasoline, and baseball caps. They are a vital link between producer and consumer.

Short-haul truck drivers stay pretty close to their home base. They may only make pickups and deliveries in one city. Or they may make day trips to nearby locations and return home the same day. A short-haul produce driver, for exam-ple, might load up in the morning and then deliver fresh fruits or eggs to several different markets throughout the day. A truck driver working for a furniture store would make several trips to the store to load furniture for delivery to peo-ple's homes. Some local drivers are responsible for product sales as well. Examples would be a bakery or soft drink driver who sells and refills products to different stores.

Long-haul drivers drive the big rigs that transport goods across state lines. They can be away from home for weeks at

a time. Companies sometimes use two drivers on especially long hauls. One driver drives while the other sleeps in a special sleeping area behind the cab. That way the truckers only have to stop for food and fuel.

There is more to being a truck driver than just sitting behind the wheel. The driver is responsible for maintaining the rig. Before taking off for a trip, the driver makes sure the truck is ready to roll by checking brakes, windshield wipers, lights, and safety equipment. It often proves helpful if a truck driver can perform some basic maintenance and repair work as well—just in case something goes wrong while on the road. The truck driver may also be responsible for helping to load and secure the cargo.

Of course, it also helps to have a good sense of direction. Truckers may be responsible for mapping out their own routes, or they may receive directions from a dispatcher at the trucking company. Gathering up-to-date reports on road conditions and weather patterns can make the difference between smooth sailing and disaster.

Long-haul drivers are usually paid by the mile but can be paid based on a percentage of the revenue their cargo brings in. Either way there's no time to waste, especially if the cargo

is perishable. However, safety can never be sacrificed for time. It is the number-one concern for truck drivers (and the other drivers who share the road with them!). Knowing when to stop and rest and staying cool, calm, and collected under even the most stressful driving conditions are valuable traits for truck drivers. For those who can't seem to control their own behavior, a national database permanently records all driving violations made by truckers. Needless to say, truckers who want to keep their jobs avoid getting their names on this list.

States require that truck drivers have to be at least 18 years old, but the Department of Transportation governs interstate commerce (business between states) and requires drivers to be at least 21. Drivers must obtain a commercial driver's license (CDL) if they drive trucks designed to carry 26,000 pounds or more. To do so, they have to pass a written test and show that they can safely operate a commercial vehicle. They also have to pass a physical examination every two years and are subject to random drug and alcohol testing.

Truck drivers have to be strong and in good physical health. Their hearing has to be good enough to hear a forced whisper in one ear at not less than five feet without a hearing aid. Vision must be 20/40 or better with or without glasses or corrective lenses. Drivers have to have normal function in their arms and legs. Blood pressure cannot be high, and truck drivers cannot have epilepsy or insulin-controlled diabetes. They have to be able to read and speak English so that they can read signs, write reports, and communicate with law enforcement officials.

The most common way to prepare for a career as a truck driver is to attend a truck driver training school. Programs last for as little as five weeks and prepare students to take the CDL and give them experience driving different types of rigs. These programs include classroom and video instruction as well as behind-the-wheel instruction.

Most trucking companies look for experienced drivers, so don't expect to start driving cross-country your first day out of school. Many drivers start out working on the loading docks for companies that have long- and short-haul routes. They get experience driving the smaller trucks and receive some on-the-job training on local routes before moving up to the big rigs.

Can you imagine yourself behind the wheel of a big rig logging tens of thousands of miles each year? Try some of the following activities to see if it's a good fit for you.

TRY IT OUT

FROM POINT A TO POINT B

Figure out the fastest, most efficient way to haul a load of cargo from where you are now to a destination of your choice that is at least 2,000 miles away. First, determine your route. You can get detailed driving directions on-line at http://www.mapquest.com. Check out the road conditions for your route at http://www.roadking.com/links/roadcond.php. Since weather conditions will affect how fast you can travel, get up-to-date forecasts for the cities you'll be traveling through at http://www.nws.noaa.gov. Find out what speed traps you may run into at http://www.roadking.com/links/speed.php. You'll need to eat, gas up, and maybe sleep, so search for truck stops to visit at http://www.truck.net/trk-stop_gtwy/truckstopdir.html. Finally, since gasoline will be your biggest expense, access current fuel prices at http://www.truckinginfo.com/diesel/prices.asp.

HIT THE ROAD

Pilot your choice of 18-wheelers on Sega Dreamcast with 18-Wheeler American Pro Trucker. You will navigate your 18-wheeler loaded down with tons of cargo on a 10,000-mile journey from New York City to San Francisco. You choose the cargo (which affects speed and acceleration). The object of the game is to make it to the finish line within the allotted time without damaging your cargo—that's pretty much the objective of any truck driver! You can take time out to try a parking game where you have to navigate through a series of

turns and park in a designated place. If you don't have a Dreamcast machine, you may be able to rent one and the game at your local video store.

CHECK OUT A TRUCKING CAREER IN CYBERSPACE

You can watch the video *New Careers in Trucking* on-line at http://www.trucking.org/insideata/foundation/video/careers_video.html. The video has interviews with truckers and will give you an idea of a trucker's life. While you are on-line, check out some of these interesting websites.

- Truckline at http://www.trucking.org is the official site of the American Trucking Associations and has up-to-date trucking industry news.
- Search for trucking jobs at http://www.1800drivers.com.
- For a daily guide to the transportation industry, visit Transport News at http://www.transportnews.com.
- Learn truck-driving lingo at http://www.truckrealm.com/glossary.htm
- Visit American Trucker at http://www.trucker.com and see how much trucks are selling for. Also link to truck manufacturers and read trucking industry news.
- RoadKing Magazine at http://www.roadking.com is loaded with helpful and interesting truck driving resources.
- The Trucker's Helper at http://www.truck.net has a comprehensive database of trucking industry links.
- Find links to trucking sites about everything from jobs and insurance to truck repair and driver training at http://www.truckrealm.com.

ROADSIDE READING

Haul yourself over to your favorite library and check out some of these books on trucking.

Bourne, Miriam Anne. *A Day in the Life of a Cross-Country Trucker.* Mahwah, N.J.: Troll Associates, 1987.

Byrnes, Mike. *Barron's How to Prepare for the Cdl: Commercial Driver's License Truck Driver's Test.* Hauppauge. N.Y.: Barrons Educational Series, 1991.

Clinton, Susan. *Tractor-Trailer-Truck Driver.* Careers without College. Mankato, Minn.: Capstone Press, 1998.

Donohue, Thomas J. *Opportunities in Trucking Careers.* Lincolnwood, Ill.: NTC Publishing Group, 1999.

Evans, Larry. *Trucking: Truths & Myths. Is This $35,000–50,000 Career for You?* Sioux Falls, S. Dak.: Two Loons Press, 1997.

Russell, William. *Truckers.* New York: The Rourke Book Company, 1994.

CHECK IT OUT

American Trucking Association Foundation
660 Roosevelt Avenue
Pawtucket, Rhode Island 02860
http://www.natsofoundation.org

American Trucking Associations
2200 Mill Road
Alexandria, Virginia 22314
http://www.truckline.com

GET ACQUAINTED

Lisa Connacher, Truck Driver

CAREER PATH

CHILDHOOD ASPIRATION: To be a pilot.

FIRST JOB: Working at a fast food restaurant.

CURRENT JOB: Truck driving instructor.

20/20 VISION AND A DOUBLE DARE

If Lisa Connacher had better eyesight, this story could well be about Connacher's career as an Air Force pilot. That's what she wanted to be when she was younger. But, without perfect vision (called 20/20), you don't get to fly.

With flying out of the question, Connacher initially went on to pursue training in criminal justice, another field she found intriguing. However, she met and married her first husband, a military serviceperson, before she had a chance to graduate.

While stationed with her husband in California, Connacher came across a newspaper ad about truck driving school. Her husband laughed when she told him she wanted to enroll. He said she'd never be able to do it. It was too hard for a woman like her.

Oh yeah? Connacher decided to prove him wrong. Six months later, with a truck driver's license in hand, Connacher was ready to hit the road in an 18-wheeler.

Of course, Connacher admits that the first time behind the wheel of a truck carrying a 40-foot trailer kind of blows you away. But she says she was thrilled to get the chance and never thought she couldn't do it.

ON THE ROAD

Connacher's trucking days took her back and forth from California to five other western states, carrying everything from eggs to empty cans to lumber. She discovered that a trucker's day generally starts early. First thing on the driver's agenda is to make sure the cargo is loaded safely and securely. They must also do safety checks on their vehicles and double check routes and destinations.

The best part for Connacher was when she finally got out on the road. She loved the freedom of being on the road two to three days at a time with no one looking over her shoulder or bossing her around.

TRICKS OF THE TRADE

Following a new marriage to a fellow truck driver and the births of two children, those long drives didn't quite fit Connacher's "family plan." That's when she traded in her truck keys for a job behind a desk in the dispatch office. As dispatcher she was responsible for scheduling truck assignments, dealing with customers, and handling all the paperwork inherent to the trucking business.

While a valuable learning experience, Connacher really missed working with trucks. When she heard that a nearby truck driving school needed instructors she jumped at the chance to apply. After completing a 40-hour training course and passing written and driving tests, Connacher was licensed as an instructor through the state of California.

WOMAN IN A MAN'S WORLD

Things are starting to change, but there are still more male truck drivers than there are female. Connacher says that hasn't been a big problem for her. She's a very good driver and can keep up with the best of them. On the rare occasion when someone questions her ability to teach, she just has to get behind the wheel and show off her skill at blind side parallel parking to put the matter to rest.

As a teacher, Connacher makes sure her students, male and female alike, learn how to drive those big rigs safely and confidently. She teaches them things like shifting, turning, securing loads, coupling and uncoupling trailers, and backing up to loading docks.

A FAMILY AFFAIR

Connacher loves driving trucks. So does her husband. The two of them have big plans for going over the road together once their children are grown. At that point, they hope to hit the road for the long hauls and see the country behind the wheel of an 18-wheeler.

GET ACQUAINTED

Donna Brown,
Trucking Industry

CAREER PATH

CHILDHOOD ASPIRATION: To be a dancer.

FIRST JOB: Working at a department store in the mall.

CURRENT JOB: Vice president of MCP Transport, a transportation brokerage company.

LIKE MOTHER, LIKE DAUGHTER

Donna Brown never expected to wind up working with her mother in the trucking business. She spent a lot of time preparing to be a dancer and hoped to one day open her own studio. But that was before her social life got hopping. Dancing started taking up too much time, so she quit—just one year shy of earning her teaching credentials.

When the time came (as it comes to all) to settle down and get a job, Brown's mom helped her get a job working as a traffic clerk in a clothing apparel company. There she was responsible for processing freight bills and claims. When the company went bankrupt six months later, Brown quickly found a similar position with another company. This time it was with a company that exported heavy-duty brake parts for trucks.

The company was small with little room for promotion, so she moved on to work at a book distribution center. Her job here involved more paperwork—filing UPS claims and keeping track of overcharges and undercharges. She used a computer to prepare spreadsheets, do data entry, and compile reports for management. For a change of pace, Brown transferred with the same company to work at one of their book-

stores in California. This didn't last long, however, because she got homesick.

BACK WHERE SHE BELONGS

Back home in Tennessee, Brown found a job with a steel company that delivered orders weighing a hundred pounds or less to customers within a 75-mile radius. This job actually put her behind the wheel of a truck. When this company started having financial problems, Brown's mom invited her to join the full-time staff of a new company. Together they have built a successful transportation brokerage company.

All those other jobs provided great training for her new position. Brown said she learned something at each job that helped her at the next. She also discovered that, as one coworker put it, "she had what it takes" to make it in this business.

KEEPING THE ROADS HOT

Brown doesn't drive a truck for her job. Instead, she matches customers who have loads to haul with truckers who have trucks to haul it in. The company specializes in dry freight, so a typical load might contain building materials, heavy equipment, or retail merchandise. The company deals with about 25 loads a day—which involves at least that many trucks.

That's not as easy as it may sound. Brown has to know a lot about trucks and the best way to move different kinds of loads to do her job right. She's learned a lot through experience, but she also worked hard to complete the certification process in transportation brokerage. This certification is like an industry seal of approval, which indicates to others that Brown knows what she's doing.

LOVE IT OR LEAVE IT

Brown admits that the transportation business is one that people either love or hate. She's been surprised to discover how much she enjoys her work. It's important work too. Nothing moves in the United States without trucks. Brown, and the truckers she works with, keep everyone supplied with all kinds of products and materials.

MAKE A DETOUR THAT TAKES YOU PLACES!

Pack your bags and get ready to explore more interesting career ideas! There are endless ways to combine your skills, your interests, *and* your wanderlust with a career that's just right for you. It may be a big world out there, but there's plenty of opportunities for people who like to travel!

Go through the following lists and see what strikes your fancy. Once you find an intriguing idea or two, use the activity starting on page 147 to find out more about it.

CAREERS THAT GET AROUND

ON LAND

automobile designer
automotive engineer
army special forces officer
bus driver
dispatcher
heavy machinery operator

logistics manager
marine serviceperson
police officer
taxi driver
subway operator

AT SEA

The next list is a long one because it includes a surprising array of jobs on major cruise lines. Those big ships are like small cities on water, so just about anything you can do on dry land, you can also do at sea. Something to consider if you're looking for a little travel and adventure in your career.

accountant
aerobics instructor
baker
bartender
bookkeeper
butcher
cabin steward
carpenter
cashier
casino dealer
chef
child-care provider
coast guard serviceperson
dancer
dance teacher
deck hand
dish washer
disk jockey
diving instructor

doctor
entertainer
ferry operator
hairstylist
laundry worker
librarian
lifeguard
maintenance engineer
masseuse
merchant marine
navy SEAL
navy serviceperson
plumber
sailor
security officer
sports pro (especially in tennis
  and golf)
steward

IN THE AIR

With today's breed of supersonic jets, the world is more accessible than ever. Here are some ways to take flight with your career.

aerospace engineer
aircraft mechanic
air force serviceperson
air traffic controller
airline ticket agent
astronaut

baggage handler
flight attendant
helicopter weather reporter
meteorologist
pilot

MORE GLOBE-TROTTING IDEAS

The tourism and hospitality industry is a huge source of employment around the world. Here are some careers that keep this business moving.

bed-and-breakfast innkeepers
chef
concierge
convention center manager
corporate travel manager
director of tourism
hotel desk clerk
hotel executive housekeeper
hotel food and beverage
    manager
hotel general manager
theme park manager
travel photographer
travel writer

INFORMATION IS POWER

Mind-boggling, isn't it? There are so many great choices, so many jobs you've never heard of before. How will you ever narrow it down to the perfect spot for you?

First, pinpoint the ideas that sound the most interesting to you. Then, find out all you can about them. As you may have noticed, a similar pattern of information was used for each of the career entries featured in this book. Each entry included:

☼ a general description or definition of the career
☼ some hands-on projects that give readers a chance to actually experience a job
☼ a list of organizations to contact for more information
☼ an interview with a professional

You can use information like this to help you determine the best career path to pursue. Since there isn't room in one book to profile all these travel-related career choices, here's your chance to do it yourself. Conduct a full investigation into a travel career that interests you.

Please Note: If this book does not belong to you, use a separate sheet of paper to record your responses to the following questions.

CAREER TITLE _____

WHAT IS A _____?
Use career encyclopedias and other
resources to write a description of this
career.

TRY IT OUT
Write project ideas here. Ask your parents and your teacher
to come up with a plan.

CHECK IT OUT
List professional organizations where you can learn more
about this profession.

GET ACQUAINTED
Interview a professional in the field and summarize your findings.

DON'T STOP NOW!

GO FOR IT!

It's been a fast-paced trip so far. Take a break, regroup, and look at all the progress you've made.

1st Stop: Self-Discovery
You discovered some personal interests and natural abilities that you can start building a career around.

2nd Stop: Exploration
You've explored an exciting array of career opportunities in travel. You're now aware that your career can involve either a specialized area with many educational requirements or that it can involve a practical application of skills with a minimum of training and experience.

   At this point, you've found a couple of (or few) careers that really intrigue you. Now it's time to put it all together and do all you can to make an informed, intelligent choice. It's time to move on.

3rd Stop: Experimentation

By the time you finish this section, you'll have reached one of three points in the career-planning process.

1. **Green light!** You found it. No need to look any further. This is *the* career for you. (This may happen to a lucky few. Don't worry if it hasn't happened yet for you. This whole process is about exploring options, experimenting with ideas, and, eventually, making the best choice for you.)
2. **Yellow light!** Close, but not quite. You seem to be on the right path, but you haven't nailed things down for sure. (This is where many people your age end up, and it's a good place to be. You've learned what it takes to really check things out. Hang in there. Your time will come.)
3. **Red light!** Whoa! No doubt about it, this career just isn't for you. (Congratulations! Aren't you glad you found out now and not after you'd spent four years in college preparing for this career? Your next stop: Make a U-turn and start this process over with another career.)

Here's a sneak peek at what you'll be doing in the next section.

☀ First, you'll pick a favorite career idea (or two or three).
☀ Second, you'll snoop around the library to find answers to the 10 things you've just got to know about your future career.
☀ Third, you'll pick up the phone and talk to someone whose career you admire to find out what it's really like.
☀ Fourth, you'll link up with a whole world of great information about your career idea on the Internet (it's easier than you think).
☀ Fifth, you'll go on the job to shadow a professional for a day.

Hang on to your hats and get ready to make tracks!

#1 NARROW DOWN YOUR CHOICES

You've been introduced to quite a few travel career ideas. You may also have some ideas of your own to add. Which ones appeal to you the most?

Write your top three choices in the spaces below. (Sorry if this is starting to sound like a broken record, but . . . **if this book does not belong to you, write your responses on a separate sheet of paper.**)

1. _____
2. _____
3. _____

WRITE YOUR RESPONSES ON A SEPARATE PIECE OF PAPER

#2 SNOOP AT THE LIBRARY

Take your list of favorite career ideas, a notebook, and a helpful adult with you to the library. When you get there, go to the reference section and ask the librarian to help you find

books about careers. Most libraries will have at least one set of career encyclopedias. Some of the larger libraries may also have career information on CD-ROM.

Gather all the information you can and use it to answer the following questions in your notebook about each of the careers on your list. Make sure to ask for help if you get stuck.

TOP 10 THINGS YOU NEED TO KNOW ABOUT YOUR CAREER

1. What kinds of skills does this job require?
2. What kind of training is required? (Compare the options for a high school degree, trade school degree, two-year degree, four-year degree, and advanced degree.)
3. What types of classes do I need to take in high school in order to be accepted into a training program?
4. What are the names of three schools or colleges where I can get the training I need?
5. Are there any apprenticeship or internship opportunities available? If so, where? If not, could I create my own opportunity? How?
6. How much money can I expect to earn as a beginner? How much with more experience?
7. What kinds of places hire people to do this kind of work?
8. What is a typical work environment like? For example, would I work in a busy office, outdoors, or in a laboratory?
9. What are some books and magazines I could read to learn more about this career? Make a list and look for them at your library.
10. Where can I write for more information? Make a list of professional associations.

#3 CHAT ON THE PHONE

Talking to a seasoned professional—someone who experiences the job day in and day out—can be a great way to get the inside story on what a career is all about. Fortunately for you, the experts in any career field can be as close as the nearest telephone.

Sure it can be a bit scary calling up an adult whom you don't know. But, two things are in your favor:

1. They can't see you. The worst thing they can do is hang up on you, so just relax and enjoy the conversation.
2. They'll probably be happy to talk to you about their job. In fact, most people will be flattered that you've called. If you happen to contact someone who seems reluctant to talk, thank them for their time and try someone else.

Here are a few pointers to help make your telephone interview a success.

- ☼ Mind your manners and speak clearly.
- ☼ Be respectful of their time and position.
- ☼ Be prepared with good questions and take notes as you talk.

One more commonsense reminder: Be careful about giving out your address and DO NOT arrange to meet anyone you don't know without your parents' supervision.

TRACKING DOWN CAREER EXPERTS

You might be wondering by now how to find someone to interview. Have no fear! It's easy, if you're persistent. All you have to do is ask. Ask the right people and you'll have a great lead in no time.

A few of the people to ask and sources to turn to are

Your parents. They may know someone (or know someone who knows someone) who has just the kind of job you're looking for.

Your friends and neighbors. You might be surprised to find out how many interesting jobs these people have when you start asking them what they (or their parents) do for a living.

Librarians. Since you've already figured out what kinds of companies employ people in your field of interest, the next step is to ask for information about local employers. Although it's a bit cumbersome to use, a big volume called *Contacts Influential* can provide this kind of information.

Professional associations. Call or write to the professional associations you discovered in Activity #1 a few pages back and ask for recommendations.

Chambers of commerce. The local chamber of commerce probably has a directory of employers, their specialties, and their phone numbers. Call the chamber, explain what you are looking for, and give the person a chance to help the future workforce.

Newspaper and magazine articles. Find an article about the subject you are interested in. Chances are pretty good that it will mention the name of at least one expert in the field. The article probably won't include the person's phone number (that would be too easy), so you'll have to look for clues. Common clues include the name of the company that the expert works for, the town that he or she lives in, and if the person is an author, the name of his or her publisher. Make a few phone calls and track the person down (if long distance calls are involved, make sure to get your parents' permission first).

INQUIRING KIDS WANT TO KNOW

Before you make the call, make a list of questions to ask. You'll cover more ground if you focus on using the five w's (and the h) that you've probably heard about in your creative writing classes: Who? What? Where? When? How? and Why? For example,

1. Who do you work for?
2. What is a typical work day like for you?
3. Where can I get some on-the-job experience?
4. When did you become a _____?
   (profession)
5. How much can you earn in this profession? (But, remember it's not polite to ask someone how much *he* or *she* earns.)
6. Why did you choose this profession?

One last suggestion: Add a professional (and very classy) touch to the interview process by following up with a thank-you note to the person who took time out of a busy schedule to talk with you.

#4 SURF THE NET

With the Internet, the new information super-highway, charging full steam ahead, you literally have a world of information at your fingertips. The Internet has something for everyone, and it's getting easier to access all the time. An increasing number of libraries and schools are

offering access to the Internet on their computers. In addition, companies such as America Online and CompuServe have made it possible for anyone with a home computer to surf the World Wide Web.

A typical career search will land everything from the latest news on developments in the field and course notes from universities to museum exhibits, interactive games, educational activities, and more. You just can't beat the timeliness or the variety of information available on the Net.

One of the easiest ways to track down this information is to use an Internet search engine, such as Yahoo! Simply type in the topic you are looking for, and in a matter of seconds, you'll have a list of options from around the world. It's fun to browse—you never know what you'll come up with.

To narrow down your search a bit, look for specific websites, forums, or chatrooms that are related to your topic in the following publications:

Hahn, Harley. *Harley Hahn's Internet and Web Yellow Pages.* Berkeley, Calif.: Osborne McGraw Hill, 1999.

Turner, Marcia Layton, and Audrey Seybold. *Official World Wide Web Yellow Pages.* Indianapolis: Que, 1999.

Polly, Jean Armour. *The Internet Kids and Family Yellow Pages.* Berkeley, Calif.: Osborne McGraw Hill, 1999.

To go on-line at home you may want to compare two of the more popular on-line services: America Online and CompuServe. Please note that there is a monthly subscription fee for using these services. There can also be extra fees attached to specific forums and services, so *make sure you have your parents' OK before you sign up.* For information about America Online call 800-827-6364. For information about CompuServe call 800-848-8990. Both services frequently offer free start-up deals, so shop around.

There are also many other services, depending on where you live. Check your local phone book or ads in local computer magazines for other service options.

Before you link up, keep in mind that many of these sites are geared toward professionals who are already working in a particular field. Some of the sites can get pretty technical. Just use the experience as a chance to nose around the field, hang out with the people who are tops in the field, and think about whether or not you'd like to be involved in a profession like that.

Specific sites to look for are the following:

Professional associations. Find out about what's happening in the field, conferences, journals, and other helpful tidbits.

Schools that specialize in this area. Many include research tools, introductory courses, and all kinds of interesting information.

Government agencies. Quite a few are going high-tech with lots of helpful resources.

Websites hosted by experts in the field (this seems to be a popular hobby among many professionals). These websites are often as entertaining as they are informative.

If you're not sure where to go, just start clicking around. Sites often link to other sites. You may want to jot down notes about favorite sites. Sometimes you can even print out information that isn't copyright-protected; try the print option and see what happens.

Be prepared: Surfing the Internet can be an addicting habit! There is so much great information. It's a fun way to focus on your future.

#5 SHADOW A PROFESSIONAL

Linking up with someone who is gainfully employed in a profession that you want to explore is a great way to find out what a career is like. Following someone around while the person are at work is called "shadowing." Try it!

This process involves three steps.

1. Find someone to shadow. Some suggestions include
   ☼ the person you interviewed (if you enjoyed talking with him or her and feel comfortable about asking the person to show you around the workplace)
   ☼ friends and neighbors (you may even be shocked to discover that your parents have interesting jobs)
   ☼ workers at the chamber of commerce may know of mentoring programs available in your area (it's a popular concept, so most larger areas should have something going on)
   ☼ someone at your local School-to-Work office, the local Boy Scouts Explorer program director (this is available to girls too!), or your school guidance counselor
2. Make a date. Call and make an appointment. Find out when is the best time for arrival and departure. Make arrangements with a parent or other respected adult to go with you and get there on time.
3. Keep your ears and eyes open. This is one time when it is OK to be nosy. Ask

questions. Notice everything that is happening around you. Ask your host to let you try some of the tasks he or she is doing.

The basic idea of the shadowing experience is to put yourself in the other person's shoes and see how they fit. Imagine yourself having a job like this 10 or 15 years down the road. It's a great way to find out if you are suited for a particular line of work.

BE CAREFUL OUT THERE!

Two cautions must accompany this recommendation. First, remember the stranger danger rules of your childhood. NEVER meet with anyone you don't know without your parents' permission and ALWAYS meet in a supervised situation—at the office or with your parents.

Second, be careful not to overdo it. These people are busy earning a living, so respect their time by limiting your contact and coming prepared with valid questions and background information.

PLAN B

If shadowing opportunities are limited where you live, try one of these approaches for learning the ropes from a professional.

Pen pals. Find a mentor who is willing to share information, send interesting materials, or answer specific questions that come up during your search.

Cyber pals. Go on-line in a forum or chatroom related to the profession you're interested in. You'll be able to chat with professionals from all over the world.

If you want to get some more on-the-job experience, try one of these approaches.

Volunteer to do the dirty work. Volunteer to work for someone who has a job that interests you for a specified period of time. Do anything—filing, errands, emptying trash cans—that puts you in contact with professionals. Notice every tiny detail about the profession. Listen to the lingo they use in the profession. Watch how they perform their jobs on a day-to-day basis.

Be an apprentice. This centuries-old job training method is making a comeback. Find out if you can set up an official on-the-job training program to gain valuable experience. Ask professional associations about apprenticeship opportunities. Once again, a School-to-Work program can be a great asset. In many areas, they've established some very interesting career training opportunities.

Hire yourself for the job. Maybe you are simply too young to do much in the way of on-the-job training right now. That's OK. Start learning all you can now and you'll be ready to really wow them when the time is right. Make sure you do all the Try It Out activities included for the career(s) you are most interested in. Use those activities as a starting point for creating other projects that will give you a feel for what the job is like.

WHAT'S NEXT?

Have you carefully worked your way through all of the suggested activities? You haven't tried to sneak past anything, have you? This isn't a place for shortcuts. If you've done the activities, you're ready to decide where you stand with each career idea. So what is it? Green light? See page 164. Yellow light? See page 163. Red light? See page 162. Find the spot that best describes your response to what you've discovered about this career idea and plan your next move.

RED LIGHT

So you've decided this career is definitely not for you—hang in there! The process of elimination is an important one. You've learned some valuable career planning skills; use them to explore other ideas. In the meantime, use the following road map to chart a plan to get beyond this "spinning your wheels" point in the process.

Take a variety of classes at school to expose yourself to new ideas and expand the options. Make a list of courses you want to try.

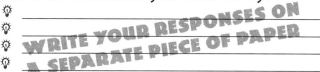

Get involved in clubs and other after-school activities (like 4-H or Boy Scout Explorers) to further develop your interests. Write down some that interest you.

Read all you can find about interesting people and their work. Make a list of people you'd like to learn more about.

Keep at it. Time is on your side. Finding the perfect work for you is worth a little effort. Once you've crossed this hurdle, move on to the next pages and continue mapping out a great future.

YELLOW LIGHT

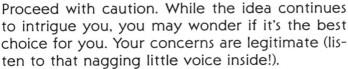

Proceed with caution. While the idea continues to intrigue you, you may wonder if it's the best choice for you. Your concerns are legitimate (listen to that nagging little voice inside!).

Maybe it's the training requirements that intimidate you. Maybe you have concerns about finding a good job once you complete the training. Maybe you wonder if you have what it takes to do the job.

At this point, it's good to remember that there is often more than one way to get somewhere. Check out all the choices and choose the route that's best for you. Use the following road map to move on down the road in your career planning adventure.

Make two lists. On the first, list the things you like most about the career you are currently investigating. On the second, list the things that are most important to you in a future career. Look for similarities on both lists and focus on careers that emphasize these similar key points.

CAUTION

Current Career	Future Career
☼ _____	☼ _____
☼ _____	☼ _____

What are some career ideas that are similar to the one you have in mind? Find out all you can about them. Go back through the exploration process explained on pages 151 to 160 and repeat some of the exercises that were most valuable.

☼ _____

☼ _____

☼ _____

☼ _____

WRITE YOUR RESPONSES ON A SEPARATE PIECE OF PAPER

Visit your school counselor and ask him or her which career assessment tools are available through your school. Use these to find out more about your strengths and interests. List the date, time, and place for any assessment tests you plan to take.

WRITE YOUR RESPONSES ON A SEPARATE PIECE OF PAPER

What other adults do you know and respect to whom you can talk about your future? They may have ideas that you've never thought of.

WRITE YOUR RESPONSES ON A SEPARATE PIECE OF PAPER

What kinds of part-time jobs, volunteer work, or after-school experiences can you look into that will give you a chance to build your skills and test your abilities? Think about how you can tap into these opportunities.

WRITE YOUR RESPONSES ON A SEPARATE PIECE OF PAPER

GREEN LIGHT

Yahoo! You are totally turned on to this career idea and ready to do whatever it takes to make it your life's work. Go for it!

Find out what kinds of classes you need to take now to prepare for this career. List them here.

WRITE YOUR RESPONSES ON A SEPARATE PIECE OF PAPER

What are some on-the-job training possibilities for you to pursue? List the company name, a person to contact, and the phone number.

- ☼ _____
- ☼ _____
- ☼ _____
- ☼ _____

Find out if there are any internship or apprenticeship opportunities available in this career field. List contacts and phone numbers.

- ☼ _____
- ☼ _____
- ☼ _____
- ☼ _____

What kind of education will you need after you graduate from high school? Describe the options.

- ☼ _____
- ☼ _____
- ☼ _____
- ☼ _____

No matter what the educational requirements are, the better your grades are during junior and senior high school, the better your chances for the future.

Take a minute to think about some areas that need improvement in your schoolwork. Write your goals for giving it all you've got here.

- ☼ _____
- ☼ _____
- ☼ _____
- ☼ _____

Where can you get the training you'll need? Make a list of colleges, technical schools, or vocational programs. Include addresses so that you can write to request a catalog.

WRITE YOUR RESPONSES ON A SEPARATE PIECE OF PAPER

HOORAY! YOU DID IT!

This has been quite a trip. If someone tries to tell you that this process is easy, don't believe it. Figuring out what you want to do with the rest of your life is heavy stuff, and it should be. If you don't put some thought (and some sweat and hard work) into the process, you'll get stuck with whatever comes your way.

You may not have things planned to a T. Actually, it's probably better if you don't. You'll change some of your ideas as you grow and experience new things. And, you may find an interesting detour or two along the way. That's OK.

The most important thing about beginning this process now is that you've started to dream. You've discovered that you have some unique talents and abilities to share. You've become aware of some of the ways you can use them to make a living—and, perhaps, make a difference in the world.

Whatever you do, don't lose sight of the hopes and dreams you've discovered. You've got your entire future ahead of you. Use it wisely.

SOME FUTURE DESTINATIONS

Wow! You've really made tracks during this whole process. Now that you've gotten this far, you'll want to keep moving forward to a great future. This section will point you toward some useful resources to help you make a conscientious career choice (that's just the opposite of falling into any old job on a fluke).

IT'S NOT JUST FOR NERDS

The school counselor's office is not just a place where teachers send troublemakers. One of its main purposes is to help students like you make the most of your educational opportunities. Most schools will have a number of useful resources, including career assessment tools (ask about the Self-Directed Search Career Explorer or the COPS Interest Inventory—these are especially useful assessments for people your age). There may also be a stash of books, videos, and other helpful materials.

Make sure no one's looking and sneak into your school counseling office to get some expert advice!

AWESOME INTERNET CAREER RESOURCES

Your parents will be green with envy when they see all the career planning resources you have at your fingertips. Get ready to hear them whine, "But they didn't have all this stuff when I was a kid." Make the most of these cyberspace opportunities.

- Future Scan includes in-depth profiles on a wide variety of career choices and expert advice from their "Guidance Gurus." Check it out at http://www.futurescan. com.
- For up-to-the-minute news on what's happening in the world of work, visit *Career Magazine*'s website at http://www.careermag.com.
- Monster.com, one of the web's largest job search resources, hosts a site called Monster Campus at http://campus.monster.com. There are all kinds of career information, college stuff, and links to jobs, jobs, jobs!
- Find links to all kinds of career information at http://careerplanning.about.com. You'll have to use your best detective skills to find what you want, but there is a lot of good information to be found on this site.

- ☿ Even Uncle Sam wants to help you find a great career. Check out the Department of Labor's *Occupational Outlook Handbook* for in-depth information on approximately 250 occupations at http://www.bls.gov/ocohome.htm.
- ☿ Buffalo State University hosts an exceptionally good career exploration website. Find it at http://www.ub-careers.buffalo.edu.career.
- ☿ Another fun site for the inside scoop on a wide variety of career options is found at http://www.jobprofiles.com.
- ☿ Pick a favorite career and find out specific kinds of information such as wages and trends at http://www.acinet.org.

IT'S NOT JUST FOR BOYS

Boys and girls alike are encouraged to contact their local version of the Boy Scouts Explorer program. It offers exciting on-the-job training experiences in a variety of professional fields. Look in the white pages of your community phone book for the local Boy Scouts of America program.

MORE CAREER BOOKS FOR GLOBE-TROTTERS

There's a world of ways to enjoy earning a living using travel-related skills. See what some of these books have to say about a career in travel:

———————

Careers in Focus: Travel and Hospitality. Chicago: J.G. Ferguson Publishing, 2000.

Hawks, John K. *Career Opportunities in Travel and Tourism.* New York: Facts On File, 1995.

Krannich, Ronald L., and Caryl Rae Krannich. Jobs for People Who Love to Travel: Opportunities at Home and Abroad. Manassas, Va.: Impact Publications, 1999.

Milne, Robert Scott. *Opportunities in Travel Careers.* Lincolnwood, Ill.: VGM Career Horizons, 1996.

Plawin, Paul. *Careers for Travel Buffs and Other Restless Types.* Lincolnwood, Ill.: VGM Career Horizons, 1991.

What Can I Do Now? Preparing for a Career in Travel and Hospitality. Chicago: J.G. Ferguson Publishing, 1998.

HEAVY-DUTY RESOURCES

Career encyclopedias provide general information about a lot of professions and can be a great place to start a career search. Those listed here are easy to use and provide useful information about nearly a zillion different jobs. Look for them in the reference section of your local library.

Cosgrove, Holli, ed. *Career Discovery Encyclopedia: 2000 Edition.* Chicago: J.G. Ferguson Publishing Company, 2000.

Hopke, William. *Encyclopedia of Careers and Vocational Guidance.* Chicago: J.G. Ferguson Publishing Company, 1999.

Maze, Marilyn, Donald Mayall, and J. Michael Farr. *The Enhanced Guide for Occupational Exploration: Descriptions for the 2,800 Most Important Jobs.* Indianapolis: JIST Works, 1995.

VGM's Career Encyclopedia. Lincolnwood, Ill.: VGM Career Books, 1997.

FINDING PLACES TO WORK

Use resources like these to find your way around the travel industry. They include lists of employers and organizations that offer opportunities for people with an interest in travel jobs.

Bell, Arthur H. *Great Jobs Abroad.* New York: McGraw-Hill, 1997.

Directory of Jobs and Careers Abroad. Princeton, N.J.: Peterson's Publishing, 1997.

Hempshell, Mark. *Getting a Job in Europe: How to Find Short or Long Term Employment Throughout Europe.* Oxford, England: How To Books, 2000.

———. *Working in Hotels and Catering: How to Find Great Employment Opportunities Worldwide.* Oxford, England: How To Books, 1997.

Hubbs, Clayton A., and Susan Griffith. *Work Abroad: The Complete Guide to Finding a Job Overseas.* Amherst, Mass.: Transitions Abroad Publishing, 1999.

Jones, Roger. *Getting a Job Abroad: The Handbook for the International Job Seeker.* Oxford, England: How To Books, 2000.

Kocher, Erik, and Nina Segal. *International Jobs: Where They Are and How to Get Them.* Reading, Mass.: Addison Wesley Longman, 1999.

Krannich, Ronald L., and Caryl Rae Krannich. *International Jobs Directory: A Guide to Over 1001 Employers.* Manassas, Va.: Impact Publications, 1999.

Landes, Michael. *The Back Door Guide to Short-Term Job Adventures: Internships, Extraordinary Experiences, Seasonal Jobs, Volunteering and Work Abroad.* Berkeley, Calif.: Ten Speed Press, 2000.

Mueller, Nancy. *Work Worldwide: International Career Strategies for the Adventurous Job Seeker.* Emeryville, Calif.: Avalon Travel, 2000.

Roberts, Elisabeth, and Jonathan Packer. *The Directory of Jobs and Careers Abroad.* Oxford, England: Vacation-Work, 2000.

Sanborn, Robert, and Cheryl Matherly. *How to Get a Job in Europe.* Chicago: Surrey Books, 1999.

Also consult the Job Bank series (Holbrook, Mass.: Adams Media Group). Adams publishes separate guides for Atlanta, Seattle, and many major points in between. Ask your local librarian if the library has a guide for the biggest city near you.

FINDING PLACES TO PRACTICE JOB SKILLS

An apprenticeship is an official opportunity to learn a specific profession by working side by side with a skilled professional. As a training method, it's as old as the hills, and it's making a comeback in a big way because people are realizing that doing a job is simply the best way to learn a job.

An internship is an official opportunity to gain work experience (paid or unpaid) in an industry of interest. Interns are more likely to be given entry-level tasks but often have the chance to rub elbows with people in key positions within a company. In comparison to an apprenticeship, which offers very detailed training for a specific job, an internship offers a broader look at a particular kind of work environment.

Both are great ways to learn the ropes and stay one step ahead of the competition. Consider it dress rehearsal for the real thing!

Anselm, John. *The Yale Daily News Guide to Internships.* New York: Kaplan, 1999.

Oakes, Elizabeth H. *Ferguson's Guide to Apprenticeship Programs.* Chicago: J. G. Ferguson Publishing Company, 1998.

Oldman, Mark. *America's Top Internships.* New York: Princeton Review, 1999.

Peterson's Internships 2000. Princeton, N.J.: Peterson's Guides, 1999.

NO-COLLEGE OCCUPATIONS

Some of you will be relieved to learn that a college degree is not the only route to a satisfying, well-paying career. Whew! If you'd rather skip some of the schooling and get down to work, here are some books you need to consult.

Abrams, Kathleen S. *Guide to Careers Without College.* Danbury, Conn.: Franklin Watts, 1995.

Corwen, Leonard. *College Not Required: 100 Great Careers That Don't Require a College Degree.* New York: Macmillan, 1995.

Farr, J. Michael. *America's Top Jobs for People Without College Degrees.* Indianapolis: JIST Works, 1998.

Unger, Harlow G. *But What If I Don't Want to Go to College?: A Guide to Successful Careers through Alternative Education.* New York: Facts On File, 1998.

INDEX

Page numbers in **boldface** indicate main articles. Page numbers in *italics* indicate photographs.